Looking for Prince Charming

Iris Leach

CRIMSON
ROMANCE
Avon, Massachusetts

This edition published by
Crimson Romance
an imprint of F+W Media, Inc.
10151 Carver Road, Suite 200
Blue Ash, Ohio 45242

www.crimsonromance.com

ISBN 10: 1-4405-5191-X
ISBN 13: 978-1-4405-5191-8
eISBN 10: 1-4405-5188-X
eISBN 13: 978-1-4405-5188-8

Dedication

FOR MY KIDS

AND MICHAEL, OUR LOST ANGEL

CHAPTER ONE

"Coffee?" Edoardo Pisani asked the tall, lean man spread out in a large chair opposite him.

"Yes, nice," George Bellows answered.

Edoardo poured coffee, placed a mug in front of George and took his seat behind his desk. "Okay, I'll bite. Why the urgency of this meeting and so early in the morning? Not like you to be up and about before eleven." He chuckled. "Politicians like the night, or so I'm told."

George guffawed. "And lawyers bill their clients for irrelevant information, or so I'm told."

The men laughed in pleasant solidarity. "What's up, George?"

George placed his coffee mug on the desk, leaned forward, and said earnestly, "I want you to campaign for mayor."

Edoardo spluttered his coffee. "What? Lord Mayor of Melbourne? Me?" He knew George, Local Member of Parliament and ex-officio of Melbourne Council, carried weight with the council; it was his pet project.

"Don't play the innocent. I know you want this, Edoardo, and I believe you'd make the perfect mayor," he said. "You're honest, you play fair, and you're the best at what you do. Heck, how many times have we talked about what you'd do for Melbourne if you had the chance? I know you'd campaign on the issues of city safety, youth homelessness, economic development ..."

"And traffic management issues," Edoardo finished, pleased that George considered him the right material for Lord Mayor of Melbourne. "I can't deny that the job doesn't interest me. Do you think the City of Melbourne would elect me?"

"By popular mandate," George said. "There's one little problem."

Edoardo sighed. "Isn't there always. Okay. 'Fess up. What's the problem?"

"Your personal life. You're like Jekyll and Hyde. You're split in the sense that your professional life is above censure but your personal life is, well, questionable."

Edoardo pulled back. George had never before reproached him about how he conducted his private life. And no matter what, Edoardo had no intention of changing a thing. He liked his life the way it was. He was in control and he meant to keep in control.

"That's got nothing to do with how I'd run the mayor's office."

"It's got everything to do with it."

Edoardo frowned. "Hell, George, next you'll be telling me what to wear."

George held up one hand. "Hear me out. You're a man of the night, Edoardo. You have a different girl on your arm every time I see you. The press would play it to the hilt, they'd murder you, and it wouldn't help the Melbourne Council. Since that fiasco about restricting car-parking in the CBD and the land tax rise, they're struggling to regain their good image." He studied Edoardo. "You've got to settle down."

Settle down? Was George joking? Sophia leaped into his mind. *Don't go down that path.* He pushed back the painful memories.

"I couldn't handle marriage, it gives me the chills just thinking about it."

Get married? How about swan diving off Uluru without feet straps? He was safe in his myriad of women and never, ever got involved. If things got out of his control and the girl had wedding bells sounding off in her ears, he'd send flowers and an expensive gift. Wish her the best for her future and cross her out of his little black book. Figuratively speaking.

He did what he did best — work. Work he understood and he could control.

"Marriage can be nice and love quietens down over the years into something really special."

"Is that a fact, George?" He shook his head. "I like my freedom. I like to pick and choose the women I go out with. No hassles, no promises, just a kiss hello and a kiss goodbye."

"And when you grow old, what then, Edoardo?"

Edoardo frowned. One woman in his life, telling him what colour tie to wear with what suit, how green vegetables grow hair on his chest and alcohol hardened arteries? No way.

Lonely old age? He'd get a dog.

"I'll worry about that in thirty years or so," he said. "No, George, marriage is not for me."

"And yet," George said, "marriage is the only thing that suits you." He sighed. "Look, Edoardo, I've known you since you first came to Australia as a kid. I'm a good friend of your parents and you."

The first tug of uneasiness niggled Edoardo. "Something bad's coming, I can feel it."

Hands on his knees, his expression serious, George said, "You won't make it as mayor without a steady relationship, and that's a fact. The only people you'll please are women under thirty. The rest will think you frivolous and too carefree for such a responsible position."

Edoardo pulled himself erect, his blood chilling, his mind freezing over. "My God, George, you're telling me to find a wife?" He tugged his tie, now as tight as a hangman's noose.

"What I'm saying is for you to get into a stable relationship. Find a nice girl who'll be by your side at all official functions. A girl that represents marriage, kids, and stability," he said. "Show Melbourne and the council that you're a steady type of bloke, ready to face and resolve any challenge the role of mayor might throw your way."

Edoardo slumped back against his chair. His perfect life quavered before his eyes before it flew out the office window and committed hara-kiri. "I don't have to marry her, do I, George? You know how I feel about marriage. I couldn't hack it."

George ignored his outburst. "Find a suitable girl from your list of women. Put things right," he paused. "We start campaigning in a month." George stood and held out his hand. "I want you as mayor, Edoardo, don't let me down."

Edoardo stood and shook George's hand. He owed this man so much. It'd been difficult for his parents when they first arrived from Italy. After buying the land in Yarra Valley and, starting the vineyard, they didn't have much time for their young son. So George had been there for him, encouraging him to study hard at school, cheering when he went to law school, patting him on the back when he opened his practice and the major success that followed.

And he honestly wanted to be mayor. He had a yearning towards politics he hadn't quite touched upon and this was his big chance. He folded his hands behind his head, leaning back in his chair staring at the ceiling. Did he know any nice girls?

What about Cindi? Hell no, she was a belly dancer at Fernando's nightclub. okay, think. Betty? His shoulders heaved. She was a mud wrestler every Friday and Saturday nights. Interesting, but definitely not what George had in mind. Who else? Mary Lou? She cooked a mean lamb roast, yes, and she'd been married four times and wasn't divorced from the last.

A stir of annoyance. Why did he have to have a nice girl anyway? Wouldn't the public accept him as a single man hell-bent on doing what was best for Melbourne? George's words echoed inside his mind, *not a man with a different girl on his arm every night.*

Edoardo lowered his head inside his hands. "Bugger, bugger, bugger," he murmured.

*

Glory Sandrin tightened the belt of her coat, hitched her bag high onto one shoulder, dug her hands deep into the pockets, and dashed up the stairs of the Empire Star building and through the main entrance.

The interior of the building was lavish. Glancing up she admired the decorative ceiling supported by columns of single pieces of Tasmanian freestone.

She ran her fingertips over the inscription on the brass plaque, Edoardo Pisani ~ Senior Counsel. One day it would read Edoardo Pisani SC and Partner.

She'd worked hard to get where she was. Part-time law school, part-time job waiting tables in a large busy restaurant in town, long hours and little pay. Then graduation with double honours and she knew the law world would be her oyster.

She hadn't counted on a workaholic like Edoardo. She now worked longer hours than uni and the cafe put together. Research, investigations, preparing legal arguments — and she loved every minute of it. Her goal was to be in the same class as Edoardo and hard work, studying him in action, was the key.

She was good. Prided herself on her cool, snap, sometimes ruthless, decisions when things weren't going the way she'd planned.

How many times had Edoardo said his practice had surged since she'd come to work with him?

She gave a friendly wave. Kate Goddard, the office law clerk, was waiting for her. Kate dressed like no other person Glory knew. Trendy cargo pants and high heels, a tight multi-coloured top that showed a little tanned skin, her hair braided into sections and hanging down over her shoulders. Bangles, beaded necklaces and a few gaudy rings completed the picture.

Dear Kate. Glory had poured her heart out to her about her childhood, the pain and sense of abandonment when her adored father had walked out on them, and the shock and grief at the sudden death of her mum. She'd told Kate her fears, her hopes, and her aspirations.

She told Kate everything, well, almost everything; there was one secret she'd kept back from her, a secret she wouldn't share with anyone because it was an impossible dream.

She was in love with Edoardo Pisani — bad-boy.

A man any sane woman would steer clear of.

Edoardo was the mirror image of her dad, the eternal womanizer. Dissatisfied with one woman they played the field, changing women as often as they changed their shirts. She could never marry a man like that. That wasn't in her master plan. "Hi, Kate."

"G'day," Kate greeted warmly. Linking arms, Kate gave her a gentle squeeze. "It's cold enough to freeze the bum off a brass monkey."

She laughed, although she chided Kate. "Prose was never your strong point."

"How'd the date go last night?"

Kate had fixed Glory up with her cousin Cameron, and, as usual, the night had turned into a disaster. "We didn't hit it off."

"You know your problem?"

Every part of her body sighed. It was far too early in the morning for Kate's psychobabble. "No, but I bet you're going to tell me."

"You're your own worst enemy. It's as if you're afraid to start a relationship."

Yes, she was scared — scared she'd make a mistake by choosing the wrong man and end up like her mum — miserable, afraid and lonely.

"He came on to me too quickly. Besides, he talked about all his conquests throughout dinner."

"He was trying to impress you."

She grimaced. "He failed miserably."

Kate chuckled. "You're twenty-six and gorgeous. A Marilyn Monroe figure and ripe for love and what do you do? Hide yourself behind dusty law books."

"I love my job," Glory protested.

"That's beside the point." Kate paused. "You're looking for Prince Charming and he only exists in fairy-tales."

"What about Greg? Isn't he your Prince Charming?"

Something dark passed over her friend's face. "Sometimes he wears his socks to bed and he burps at the dinner table."

"You're so down-to-earth." Glory wouldn't be put off. "I think the perfect man is out there somewhere and I'm going to find him."

"And then?"

She managed a smile. "We'll marry and—"

Kate's eyebrows rose and she shook her head. "And live happily ever after?"

Glory knew her Prince Charming *was* out there and she *would* find him. She just knew she would. He'd be a one-woman man, a man who would put her above all others and then all her torturous dreams of loving Edoardo would dissolve. "You sound embittered. Kate, is anything wrong?"

"Could be."

"Tell me about it."

"We'll talk later." Kate glanced over her shoulder. "Better go, got heaps of work piled on my desk. Wanna do lunch?"

"Early lunch. I'm due in court at two."

"I can eat any time." She grinned and said, "See you later." Kate made her way to her office on the opposite side of the room.

Glory poured herself a black coffee, sipped it, grimaced, added milk and sugar and returned to her chair. Rain splattered against the window, sounding like the first hesitant clack of a typewriter. Within seconds, it had gathered momentum and was thundering down like a thousand tapping feet.

Her childhood ended at fifteen when her father left. Her mother sank into a deep depression and eventually died — Glory knew it was from a broken heart. She would never be able to repay Kate for her kindness, friendship, and love.

*

The telephone rang. "Pisani ... hi, Pete, how's your little one? Over the measles yet? ... Great, glad to hear it ... Hey, you don't have to thank me. I knew you were the perfect man for the job. Only took one phone call, that's all ... The Browne file? Yes, Kate sent it Friday night; you should have got it first thing this morning ... I see ... OK, I'll call you back." He replaced the receiver.

"Hell," he muttered. "This is too much." He pressed a number on the telephone pad. "Kate? Get in here now."

Edoardo stewed while waiting for the hapless Kate. All his frustrations at George dangling the carrot beneath his nose only to whip it away, burned inside him. For the first time, in a long time, he wasn't in control and he didn't like the feeling.

Kate entered the room.

"Where's the Browne file?" Edoardo growled. "I just got a call from the Clerk of Courts." Kate's face turned a pasty green. "You forgot to send it, didn't you?"

Before Kate could answer, Edoardo, his head still reeling from George's weird request, spoke more harshly than he intended. "This isn't the first mess up, Kate. Last week you misplaced the Tyson affidavit and made me late for court. And you've been late most mornings. You know how important it was to have that file delivered. What's got into you? I've never known you to be so careless.

"The court postponed and the client still has to pay full court costs and he won't be pleased," he said. "You've caused unnecessary expense and discredited the practice."

12

"I'm sorry, Edoardo. It's just that everything fell in on me ..."
Edoardo's frustrations tightened into a ball that he tossed Kate's
way. "That doesn't cut it, Kate. I need someone I can rely on. I
don't want to have to think of every little thing. I employ you to
do a job and to be damn frank, you're not doing it. The practice
relies on all the staff doing their job and doing it well." He shook
his head. "I have to let you go, Kate. Sorry, but that's it."

"Edoardo, please."

"That's all, thanks, Kate," he said more gently now. Sanity was
returning.

As the dejected girl left his office, he reconsidered. Kate had
been with him since the beginning and Edoardo knew he couldn't
be without her. She was the best law clerk in Melbourne, and
although her style of dressing was bizarre to say the least, she
brightened up a rather dull law office and she was a lovely girl.

He ran a shaky hand over his forehead. He'd never spoken
harshly to any of his staff before and he was ashamed of his
outburst.

Poor Kate, he hadn't given her a chance to explain. Nothing so
major had happened in the past. He'd apologise to her immediately.
Explain, he'd had a rough morning and was taking it out on her.
Assure her that her job was as safe as houses.

As his hand reached out to dial Kate's extension the telephone
rang. Edoardo picked up the receiver.

*

Kate stumbled to her office, slumped into a chair and covered
her face with her hands. Her shoulders heaved. Glory jumped to
her feet, her heart pounding. Something was terribly wrong. She
raced across the office to Kate's side. Throwing her arms around
her, Glory said, "What is it? What's happened?"

Kate gave a small sob and cried, "Oh, Glory, Edoardo sacked me."

Glory stumbled back a few steps. "He what? Why? Why would he sack you? It doesn't make any sense. You're the best worker he has."

"Not according to him, I ain't. I mucked up big time. I forgot to send the Browne file to court. The trial was postponed." Kate groaned, rubbing her hands over her eyes. "I tried to explain but he was livid, angrier than I've ever seen him. Actually it's the only time I've seen him angry since I've known him. He must have personal problems."

"Don't stick up for him, Kate. He's acting like a callous brute." Glory glanced towards Edoardo's office. "And he needs to be told."

Kate grabbed Glory's hand. "I can't lose my job, Glory. I've got problems."

Glory said, "What problems? You never told me about any problems? Oh, Kate is it you? Are you ill? Is it Greg? Oh God, it's not Aiden is it? What? What!"

Kate wiped her eyes and nose with a tissue. This small act broke Glory's heart in pieces. She wanted to don armour and, with sword raised, mount her stead and fight the savage foe for her friend — the savage foe being the gorgeous Edoardo Pisani.

Kate tossed the tissue into the wastepaper basket. "Greg left me over two months ago."

Another shock trundled through Glory. "Left you? For good?"

"Yes."

"Why didn't you tell me? Why have you kept something so terrible to yourself?"

"I kept thinking I may not have to, hoping he'd come back and say he'd made a mistake." She shook her head. "He's not coming back to me, Glory."

"Why? Oh, Kate, is it another woman?"

She shrugged trembling shoulders. "I got home from work and there was this note propped against the toaster. It said: *Get a new life, I have. Good luck, Greg.*"

Angry at Greg's cold-hearted dismissal of his wife and child, Glory said, "Cold-hearted brute. Where's he gone?"

"He's in New Zealand and yes he's with another woman."

"What, you mean he's just run off and doesn't care about seeing Aidan again?"

"Yes, isn't he a rat bastard?"

"Oh my God, I never imagined he'd be the kind of man who'd do that! You'll get child support. He'll help you financially."

Kate straightened. "Too bloody right I will. I'll take the swine for every penny he's got."

"I'll represent you. Together we'll make him squirm."

"You're not a divorce lawyer."

"I'll still handle your case."

Kate squeezed Glory's hand. "I know you would, but I don't want to involve you. You're my friend, not my lawyer."

"Why didn't you explain this to Edoardo?"

"I don't want his sympathy, Glory," she said. "Don't you tell him about Greg leaving me. I don't want him keeping me on because he's sorry for me."

Glory sighed but said, "I won't, I promise. But you must promise me something."

"What?"

"Even with child support it won't be easy for you to manage financially. You know the house payments or medical bills, anything, you'll come to me."

Kate shook her head. "I can't promise you that. Borrowing money is a sure way to damage a friendship." The girls' eyes met. "I won't risk losing your friendship, Glory."

"You'd be the most mule-headed person I know." Glory grinned. "And I love you for it." She glanced again towards Edoardo's office. "I'll tell you one thing, Kate, you're not going to lose your job." She shook her head and set her lips in determination. "No way in this world."

Kate brightened. "How?"

Purpose flooded through her. Edoardo's night-time habits were questionable, but not his professional life and he usually showed more consideration than necessary towards his staff.

She recalled when Cynthia Swallow, their receptionist, found herself pregnant to a married man. Edoardo had stood by her all the way, giving her extended maternity leave and paying her wages until she was ready to return to work.

So what was going on? She found it difficult to believe that he would sack someone as important to him as Kate for no good reason.

Whatever, she was just the girl to set him right.

"I'll show you how. Just watch me in action. Edoardo Pisani is in for the shock of his pampered life."

And with that statement, she turned, tugged her skirt down over her hips, fluffed her hair and marched, like a soldier to battle, towards the enemy's office.

CHAPTER TWO

Edoardo glanced up as Glory entered his office without knocking. He mumbled an apology into the receiver and dropped it back on the cradle. "Glory, what can I do for you? You look — um, upset."

"I want to talk to you about Kate and the appalling way you spoke to her and giving her notice as if she doesn't mean a thing to you or the practice. Really, Edoardo, this is too much." A savage glare. "Why, she's crying her heart out. How can you be so uncaring, so unfeeling? It's not like you, Edoardo, not one little bit."

A denial sprang to his lips. An explanation of how he'd lost it there for a bit and had taken it out on Kate but he intended rectifying the situation. But something, stirring and wicked, held him back.

He didn't know much about Glory's personal life. Hadn't wanted to know. Best, he'd decided, to keep their relationship strictly-business. That wasn't as easy as it sounded, as right at this moment his hands were itching to touch her. Run his hands through the silk of her hair, press his mouth against hers. He'd always held back for two reasons, one, knowing she was a girl who wanted a solid gold band on the fourth finger of her left hand and two, they worked together and he didn't want to lose her. Still that didn't stop him from indulging in fantasies.

He lowered his head, his fingers pressed against his forehead. *Snap out of it, man.* "Kate messed up."

"We all mess up at times, Edoardo," she said crisply. "Want I should go though a few of yours?"

He laughed, loving her spirit, the way she always had an answer, never allowing him to dragoon her in any way, shape or form. And the idea that was budding around the back of his mind bloomed into full life.

She was a woman any man would like to have on his arm. Personally he'd like to have her in his arms, feel the softness of her body as it pressed against his.

The smell of her perfume encircled him, Bergamot or maybe mandarin and just a hint of frangipani. His senses swirled. The room closed in. He tugged the collar of his shirt and glanced at the central heating vent. Had the darn thing broken down?

"Have you a partner, Glory?" He struggled to keep his voice relatively normal. "You know, someone special in your life?"

His questions took her aback, and she said, "Partner?" She pointed to her chest. "Me? No, no, I haven't got a partner."

*

As Glory leaned in closer, she took in the man she'd been working with for the past two years. In his dark blue suit with silver gray pinstripes, a light blue cotton shirt and a dark gray woven silk tie, she decided he was well worth the scrutiny.

She'd been in love with Edoardo from the first moment she'd laid eyes on his darkly alluring presence and smouldering looks.

His figure was tall and muscular and he had the most remarkable eyes. At first she'd taken these intense orbs to be violet, but on examination they were deep blue.

If only he were a different type of man, a homebody, a family man who'd rush home each night on the 6.05 to be with her.

The only rushing Edoardo would do was into the next dolly bird's arms.

"It seems I don't know much about you," he said. "I know you're a superb lawyer. The way you give confidence to your client and handle a judge and jury is just short of brilliant."

Compliments from Edoardo Pisani were rare. "What does my

personal life have to do with how you treated Kate?"

"Can't I give you a compliment?"

"For heaven's sake, Edoardo, what are you fishing for?" she snapped.

She tried to drag her gaze away from his, but he held her with a look that so fascinating she was absorbed completely — spellbound. A sensual pull, a breathless response to him. He had all the dazzling intensity of an electric storm and just as dangerous. What was his secret to driving her crazy? Was it his deep blue eyes with the slightly devilish glint, the boyish grin flashing the startling white of his teeth or the exciting feeling that when you were with him you brushed with temptation?

With a shake of her head, she reminded herself why she was in his office, and it was certainly not to discuss her life or admire his physical attributes.

Throwing questions at her was so typical of his style. A lawyer to the death. Well, so was she and she knew how to argue a case. "About Kate and her wrongful dismissal," she began.

Again he interrupted her. "You're an orphan, aren't you, Glory?"

"Yes, I'm an orphan and I eat cereal for breakfast with the right amount of oat-bran to keep the old cholesterol down." Her voice was a flat monotone. "I exercise regularly and I clean my teeth morning and night with mint-flavoured toothpaste." She tilted her head and gave him a dead-eye stare. "Anything else you want to know?"

He grinned like a cheeky schoolboy and her heart melted and she wondered, just for a moment mind, if he was too much man for her to handle.

"I have a — um, a proposition to put to you."

She looked at him suspiciously, hunched her shoulders, and said, "A legal proposition?"

His eyes glinted with mischief. "Depends on how you look at it." He drew in a deep breath and ran his fingers through the lush of his hair. Lucky fingers. "I'm considering campaigning for Lord Mayor of Melbourne and I've been told by my campaign manager I need a nice girl by my side."

"You have a briefcase full of names and addresses, Edoardo. Give them a shuffle and take a pick. If anything you don't lack feminine company. So what's the problem?"

He smiled indulgently. "I don't know any nice girls."

He'd never choose a woman who might think about commitment, not the gorgeous hey-I'm-strictly-bachelor-material Edoardo Pisani.

"How come I'm not surprised?" she said.

His eyes softened to a warm blue as he looked at her. He was being too nice. She glanced over her shoulder at the distance between her and the office door. Hasty exit — maybe!

"Will you help me?"

The surprise at his question made her jerk back. "To find you a nice girl?"

"No, to be my nice girl."

She jumped up as if ants had bitten her. What was he suggesting? Was he asking her out on a date? The large book-cluttered office seemed to fill with awkwardness. She was shaken, she'd admit this. But she was also curious and curiosity won the day.

"What's this all about, Edoardo?" she demanded.

He slumped back against the chair, placing his hands behind his head, the buttons on his shirt threatened to pop as his muscles tightened, and his shirt stretched to tearing point. Mr Australia, eat your heart out.

"Just what I said. There's no hidden agenda." His tone suggested, *don't kid yourself, this is strictly platonic.* "I need a nice girl to be by my side until I gain office," he said casually as if he were ordering a serve of fish and chips. "The right image a prospective mayor should radiate. That's all. And I'm asking you to be that nice girl."

She flicked her hair over her shoulder, her mind a twirl of

confusion. She looked away from him and inclined her face to the rain-splattered window. "Let me get this straight in my head." She turned her face back to him. "You want me to pretend to be your girl, like pretend to be in love with you for the cameras, for your public image?" She paused. "Smile adoringly into your eyes when the press is present?"

He had the grace to look abashed. "Yes." He smiled, a rather laconic smile, and any empathy she held for him died a ghastly death. He was so darn sure of himself, it was a crime.

Be his girl? If she wanted torture she'd have her toenails pulled out, at least she could handle that pain. "That's a big ask, Edoardo."

He placed an elbow on the desk, his arched finger pressed lightly against his lower lip, he said, "Maybe, maybe not. What have you got to lose?"

He leaned towards her and, reaching over, he touched, ever so lightly, the back of her hand. She tugged her hand away with a sharp forceful pull as if it had been scorched, needing to look and see if his fingerprints had branded her skin.

He arched a brow at her. "Maybe there's something I can do for you in return."

She couldn't resist rubbing her hand, as if eradicating all trace of him. "Like what?" she challenged. "There's nothing you can give me, Edoardo." *Liar, liar, pants on fire.*

Glory's eyes met Edoardo's, focussing on the heat that flared between them. Her master plan teetered. He'd take her to his bed in a flash, with a wham bang, thank-you ma'am, and I'll give you a call sometime, goodbye. That was so not what she wanted; not from Edoardo; not from any man.

"I think there could be," he said.

He always had a comeback, always setting her back. She made a small, scornful sound. "Such as?"

"Quid pro quo, Glory. Kate's job."

"Kate's job! Kate should get her job back because you're an

idiot to fire her, not because I agree to play your girlfriend!"

"That's the deal, take it or leave it."

She wondered if she could do this and remain sane. Go out with Edoardo on dates, albeit pretend dates. Holding hands, smiling sweetly into each other's eyes. Could she trust him? He wasn't a hold-your-hand-kisses-on-the-cheek-man; he was hold-on-to-your-hat full-steam ahead-check-the bed-for-scorch-marks-man.

She wasn't made of steel and he'd think nothing of making her his latest conquest. She knew it'd take every ounce of her self-will and preservation to resist him. But resist she would. She had no intention of becoming another notch on his personal cupid's bow.

"And if I say no, then Kate loses her job." That was something she couldn't allow happen. A single parent, Kate depended on her position here and Glory would do anything to put a smile back on her friend's face.

"Yes."

Shock waves at his callous response. "You were never cruel, Edoardo."

His face told her he didn't like what she'd said. Too bad if the truth hurt.

"I'm desperate, and a desperate man uses desperate methods." He ran his fingers over his mouth. For a sweet brief moment, she imagined it locked with hers. She tingled and a shiver raced up her spine.

He pushed himself out of the chair and walked to her side. Her heart beat way too fast. "Look, Glory, there's no skin off your nose. You get a few nights at posh places. Your photo in magazines."

How could she bring him undone? "I'm not photogenic. I come out looking like a mug shot." She wished he'd move back from her. She couldn't quite get her breath.

He gave an exasperated sigh. Loud and long so there would be no misunderstanding about how he truly felt. "Come on, Glory, help me out here." He moved away from her, parking himself on the edge of his desk. Papers fluttered nervously.

Her mouth tugged down. She knew he had her cornered and he knew this as well. That was why he'd played his ace, knowing how fond she was of Kate and how she'd allow nothing, within her power, to hurt her.

Again those devilishly blue eyes twinkled like a naughty boy who knew he could charm his mum and get out of trouble scot-free.

"You never intended firing Kate, did you?"

He had the decency to look abashed. "Are you kidding? She's the best law clerk around. Man would have to be mad to let her go."

She stood. "Discussion over."

He reached out to touch her cheek. "How about I add some spice? It may change your mind about helping a bloke out."

Suspicion lingered in her mind. What was he up to now? His legal brain as sharp as a tack, well so was hers, and she was ready for anything Edoardo handed out. "And that would be?"

"I'll throw Kate an extra bonus."

"How much?"

"Ten thousand."

"On top of her bonus she receives now?"

"Yes."

Excellent, but Kate had big problems. "Not enough for all her pain and suffering. Could make good litigation out of this and come out with bells on our toes," she said. "She's worked like a dog for you since you opened this practice and personally I think she deserves a big fat bonus, don't you, Edoardo? And every year from now on."

His brows burrowed as his forehead crinkled into frown lines. "You're not in court."

She grinned. "Yet," she said sweetly.

A grin twitched the corners of his delectable mouth. How

could one man have so much? "Okay, I'll double the offer. Twenty thousand."

"And?"

"And every year from now on."

A nice bank balance for Kate for any emergency that may arise, this was a sweet deal. Well, for Kate anyhow.

She wasn't quite sure how she'd go being on a personal level with Edoardo; she didn't want to end up drooling all over his hand-made Berluti shoes. As if. "Now you're talking."

"You strike a hard bargain, Glory."

"I learnt it from you, Edoardo."

His blue eyes flashed, as he held out a big hand. "Deal?" He did a Groucho Marx thingy with his eyebrows. He was irresistible. And she couldn't help grinning. He really was so nice, so charming — sometimes. Darn shame Edoardo Pisani was Casanova reincarnated.

She stood and slid her hand inside his. Firm yet warm, tingly. Her body swayed towards his and, as he leaned forward, her mouth opened slightly as if to welcome his kiss. She drew back and lightly shook her head. "Deal," she said.

He gave her hand a light squeeze before releasing it. Adrenaline surged, which she was thankful for as she was beginning to hyperventilate at an alarming rate.

"First things first," he said. "I want you to meet my campaign manager, George Bellows, and his wife Beth. Nice people. You'll like them."

"For approval, Edoardo?"

He looked genuinely surprised. "What do you mean by that crack?"

"The okay from your campaign manager that I'm the *right* type of girl. A nice girl."

Now he was angry. His eyes blue thunder. *Well, too bad, Edoardo, you can't have it all your own way.*

"Nothing of the sort," he said. "George is a lifetime friend of my family. I want him to meet you and vice-versa."

The confusion in his voice stabbed at Glory's heart.

"Why do you twist everything I say?" he asked.

She held up her hand, pleased that she had rattled the unflappable, even if only slightly. "Okay, Okay, don't blow your top. I'll meet them."

He settled back in his chair. His gorgeously sculptured mouth pulling slightly down at the corners, made him look more irresistible, if that were possible, and an image of him, clad only in jeans, his muscular chest smoothed with oil and rippling deliciously every time he moved, flashed into her mind.

Cool down, girl.

"We'll have dinner with them tonight."

Was he kidding? She wasn't mentally prepared. She needed like about ten years or so. "Tonight?" she spluttered. "I'm not sure about tonight."

He laughed softly the oh-so-sure-of-himself Edoardo now back and confident of his ability to charm her. "And that would be because—?"

"I've got so much work to do," she muttered. "I need to catch up."

"That's never stopped you before. You've dropped work at a minute's notice when it's been a business dinner."

Her nostrils flared with irritation. If she concentrated she could dislike Edoardo intensely. All it needed was self-will and deep mental yoga.

"Tonight is fine."

He was laughing at her. She could see it in his eyes and in the twitching of his mouth and her frustration and anger grew.

"Great, I'll pick you up at seven."

"I can meet you at the restaurant, if you like."

He gave her a thunderous look. "I never allow women to meet

me at restaurants." And that was that.

He sat back at his desk, head down; meeting finished, and like lamb to slaughter Glory left his office.

CHAPTER THREE

Glory took ages to get ready. Her bed was laden with cast off clothes as she searched for the perfect outfit. She told herself she was trying to impress George Bellows and his wife, but deep down she knew she wanted to throw Edoardo back on his heels, make him sit up and take notice.

For work she wore top designer suits like Prada, Versace, and Cavalli and, of course, Armani. A suit was professional, classy, and elegant. A suit screamed power, competence, and ambition, an image she strived for and had succeeded in attaining.

Tonight she wanted a different look. Tonight she wanted to look feminine, sexy, and chic.

Dating Edoardo?

She couldn't believe it was happening. Yet the relief and smiles from Kate was worth it. She'd tried to corner Glory with endless questions. What had she said to make Edoardo change his mind? What had Edoardo said? And why, after giving Kate the royal order of the boot had he offered the extraordinarily yummy bonus?

Glory had mumbled something about Edoardo realising his mistake and wanting to make amends. That he had acted in haste.

She knew Kate was far from finished. That she did indeed intend to cross-examine. There would be more grilling until Kate wormed the truth from her.

The front door bell rang, and she swallowed down the tiny surge of apprehension that floated up into her throat. She wouldn't allow Edoardo, or any man, to unnerve her.

She'd fought all savage foes and had come out a winner; so one big gorgeous hunk of a bloke with electric blue eyes and a mouth that Pablo Picasso would give his last paintbrush to capture on canvas wasn't any more to her than a jumping flea in a teacup.

Confidence restored, she took one last look in the mirror, a fluff of her hair, maybe a touch more lipstick, and da dah ready or not here comes Glory.

Edoardo stood there and smiled his dimpled smile, and everything dissolved into the background. He was handsome and strong and so virile he made her blood bubble.

He wore a black moleskin jacket, cream business shirt with a dark gray and black striped tie, and gray gabardine trousers. He looked tough but sensitive.

For a brief moment they measured each other, and then he leaned forward and lowered his voice intriguingly. "You look lovely."

She glanced down at what she was wearing. A cream and silver vertical stripe pants-suit, but with a feminine touch under the jacket, a silk/satin waistcoat on bare skin. She'd always felt good in this suit, and knew it was most suitable for dinner.

He leaned in closer. Her heart thumped crazily in her chest. His smell overpowered her; cedar wood aftershave, citrus soap, totally male odours.

And when he kissed her softly on the mouth, an affectionate kiss, not the passion she so craved from him, yet she was rendered nonoperational, a limp version of her former self.

"You kissed me." She touched her lips with her fingers.

"Let's try it again and this time you kiss me back," he said.

She didn't argue and when his mouth connected with hers, she pressed hard against his mouth. She opened her lips slightly and explored with the tip of her tongue. They broke apart, breathing heavily. She'd been kissed before but never quite like this.

"That's better," he said softly.

The breath had all but left her body. She breathed deeply through her nostrils. She loved him so darn much. If only he didn't play the field. If only he wanted to settle down, marry, and have kids. If only …

"Want a drink before we go?"

He glanced at his watch and shook his head. "Maybe when we get back?"

Like that was going to happen; sitting in front of a roaring fire, sipping wine, swapping work stories, kissing. Her resistance towards him was at an all-time low.

He reminded her of the dark handsome prince from fairy-tales of her childhood. The prince who always rescued the princess from danger; who'd sweep her up onto his white steed and ride her away to his castle in the clouds; the prince who always kissed the princess and whispered his love on promises of happily-ever-after.

Edoardo Pisani was a fairy-tale prince scared of commitment. Not for the first time she wondered why he was. What had happened that made him a serial womanizer? The perpetual bachelor? What was that touch of sadness deep in his eyes? Had he been hurt in the past?

She longed to know the Edoardo Pisani story.

In the practice he was sweet, understanding of his staff's needs, taking time to listen and help wherever he could. She liked his gentleness, his humour, his compassion, and the way he gave his full attention to whomever was speaking to him. This kind-heartedness had attracted her to him in the first place.

In court, he was ruthless. Once Edoardo believed his client was innocent — that was the only way he'd accept a case and this was her ruling too — he let nothing stand in his way of success.

In her mind's eye he was standing in front of the jury box, belting out his closing address, the way his muscles rippled across his back as he waved his hands for effect. His spread-eagle stance, arms on slim hips, shoulders broad and strong, and his brilliant blue eyes sparkling with triumph he knew was already his.

She hardened her heart and took a silent resolve not to allow this man's magic to twist her emotions. She told herself that she would remain constantly alert and in control of the situation, no matter what happened.

"I'll get my coat and bag," she said.

He moved inside the apartment but stood, as if ready for a quick exit, near the front door. When she returned he said, "My car's parked around the corner."

He placed his hand lightly on her back, guiding her out the front door, down the elevator, out the main doors, down the street towards the parked car. In the growing dusk, a wind played leapfrog with his thick thatch of black hair. The warmth of his fingers pressing lightly on her back radiated the length of her spine. It was as if he had fire in his fingertips.

A leopard didn't change his spots and all the lamenting and hoping that he could be different was only a pipe-dream. He was a man who played the field, same as her dad, one woman wasn't enough for them and they didn't care who they hurt in their desire to appease their ego. Men like Edoardo and her dad should never marry, never tie themselves to one woman. It only led to heartache for the woman.

So remember what this is all about. They had made a deal. Edoardo had stuck to his side of the bargain, now she was obliged to stick to hers.

He opened the car door for her. He slid in beside her. With a flick of a key the big engine of the super-smooth pure black BMW purred into life.

Edoardo decisively edged his way into the line of traffic and, within minutes they were at the restaurant. They entered a foyer ablaze with light and colour. A tidal wave of chattering voices and the clinking of glass and silver engulfed them. A waiter, in black evening dress, hurried towards them. "Pisani, for four."

The waiter gave a small nod. "Your table's ready, sir." He led them to a dark and secluded table at the far side of the restaurant.

Glory noted all the women's eyes followed him. Fascinated

by his build, the thickness of his coal black hair and dark blue, meaningful eyes.

The waiter hovered at Edoardo's side. "Would you care for a drink?"

"What would you like to drink?" Edoardo asked.

"White wine would be nice."

Without looking at the wine list, Edoardo spoke to the waiter. "A bottle of your best Sauvignon Blanc." He waited until the waiter had left.

She tried to guess what he was thinking, but his lids were heavy, shading his eyes, and with the muted light of the restaurant, Edoardo seemed far too fascinating for her own sanity.

"Tell me about yourself."

She shrugged, folding her hands in her lap. "What's to tell?"

He gave her a careful look. "What do you do in your spare time?"

She feigned shock. "What spare time? You work me to death."

He chuckled, folded his arms, and focussed his attention on Glory. "Well," he said, "I know you do a lot of Legal Aid work."

She eyeballed him. "Don't be ingenuous, Edoardo, so do you."

"Touché! Okay, what do you do when you're not being worked to death?"

Someone was tinkling out a sweet tune on a piano. She recognized the tune but couldn't put a name to it. She understood him wanting to know about her personal life. After all, she was his *girl*, and he'd look a right dork if someone asked something about her and he hadn't a clue how to answer. She wasn't kidding herself that he really wanted to know about her. Heck, she'd take a bet that he didn't know a thing about any of his harem except their name, rank and serial number.

"Um, I adore the theatre, and I mean movies too. I love going to the pictures." She shrugged, screwed the corner of her napkin into a tight wad, and said, "I play a little golf and tennis. I like to lie on the beach and eat chocolate ice cream, and I love the great romantic poets, Tennyson and Wordsworth, Elizabeth Barrett Browning."

"How do I love thee? Let me point the way," he recited crisply.

Glory hesitated, wondering if he was deliberately misquoting. "It's count the ways."

One dark eyebrow shot up and he looked genuinely surprised. "Excuse me?"

Oh My God! He'd actually made a genuine mistake. She was pleased she'd found a flaw, as she was beginning to suspect he was absolutely perfect. "You said point and the correct quote is: How do I love thee? Let me count the ways."

He gave a sexy smile and there was a look in his eyes that made her burn inside. Her heart jumped a beat.

"Yes, right, count the ways."

They laughed and she found herself relaxing in his company.

The waiter returned with their wine and poured a little glittering pale yellow liquid into Edoardo's glass. He tasted it.

"Hmm, that's fine," he said. Edoardo waited while the waiter poured the wine into her glass, top his, and then raising his glass to her, he nodded and said, "Here's to adventure."

She raised her glass. "Adventure," she chorused, and sipped her wine. "It's delicious." She twirled the stem of her glass, glanced at him through lowered lashes. There wasn't anything about this man she didn't like. She liked his hair, his physique, his eyes — she shifted uncomfortably in her seat — make that she loved his eyes. They were cheeky boy eyes. Eyes that made you forgive the crime before he'd even committed it. If she'd had him especially made to order, he couldn't be more wonderful. Just what the doctor ordered.

And for all her self-talk and recriminations, she knew that if Edoardo kissed her again she'd kiss him back without caring about the consequences.

She glanced at him just as he was licking his lips from the wine. Fascinated as the tip of his tongue ran the full extent of his upper lip and then along the lower. A quick rush of excitement. Heat flared in her cheeks.

Here she went losing control of her emotions five seconds after being in his company. *Shape up, girl.* She reached for her glass and tossed down the wine in one long swig. She closed her eyes as the sweet liquid flowed down her throat, and enter her bloodstream. Edoardo topped her glass. She smiled her thanks.

She'd handled some of the toughest cases in Australia and had never as much as been stressed out. She'd argued with high-court judges about rulings, barristers speaking on their client's behalf and waiters about the price of fish. She'd sat on panels and answered improbable questions from eager young law students. She'd been interviewed on *Stark Reality* and won the heart of Lew Myers, the hard-hitting news interviewer who, as far as Glory could tell, didn't like his own mother.

So to allow a man who couldn't remember the woman he took out last night bedazzle her? No way ho-say.

His mobile phone rang. "Excuse me," he said as he took the call. "Pisani ... Okay ... Sure, that's fine." He clicked the mobile shut. "That was George. There's trouble with the babysitter, she couldn't make it. They've rung an agency and another should be there in an hour or so. He said for us to eat and they'll meet us here for coffee and drinks." The waiter placed a menu in front of him. "Is there anything you especially like?"

"I like all Italian food," she enthused.

"Would you like me to order or would that offend your feminine principles?"

"I'll give way to your male ego." At his frown, she grinned. Reaching for her glass, she took a deep gulp of wine and her head spun. If she kept attacking her wine in this way she'd be tipsy, and she wanted to be in full control of her mind. She pushed the glass a little way from her. Only sips from now on.

He gave the waiter their order, and handed him back the menu. "And some bruschetta," he added quickly. "Were you born in Melbourne, Glory?"

"New South Wales, in Bateman's Bay. It's a pretty holiday town at the mouth of the Clyde River, and the closest beach resort to Canberra."

"I'd like to go there one day."

She'd like to take him there. "The bay is renowned for its crayfish and oysters."

He gave her a steady look. Glory blew out a breath. He was totally hot. "Why did you leave Bateman's Bay?"

She pulled her head back, studying him. "Are you grilling me, Edoardo? I feel like I'm in the witness box." She laughed and continued. "My mother came to Melbourne when I was fifteen."

The waiter placed plates of steaming food in front of them. Linguini with clam sauce. One of her favourite dishes. She toyed with her food. Thinking of her mother made all earlier traces of hunger evaporate.

As they reached over for bread, his fingers lightly brushed her hand, and a shock of electricity raced up her arm and pierced her heart. An image, so vivid of his mouth on hers, flashed into her mind. She blushed hot and long, her stomach churning.

"More wine?" he asked. She shook her head, studying the strength of his hands as he poured wine into his glass. "You're not eating."

"I ate too much lunch."

His eyes scrutinized her and she knew that look, had seen it a thousand times in court. The look just before the criminal confessed and threw himself on the mercy of the court.

"You're not on one of those perpetual diets, are you? That drives me crazy."

She grinned. "No, just naturally thin."

He placed one elbow on the table, cupping his chin in his hand, leaning towards her, ever so close. *My God, his eyes are so blue.* She swallowed harshly.

"Hmmm, I wonder."

"Hey, I'll put on weight."

He smiled that lethal smile. Surely there was a police warrant out on it? "Not too much."

"No, not too much." She enjoyed the gentle sparring as much as he did. His eyes shone with good humour. "I intend to finish up with strawberry cheesecake and chocolate ice cream. Calories are my best friend."

He threw back his dark head and laughed. It was a lovely deep chuckle that warmed her heart. An odd aching pain built up inside her, and she realized she was out of her emotional depth with a man like Edoardo, that his sheer sexuality swamped her until she couldn't tell her left foot from her right.

Their conversation became light and easy. The Bellows arrived with apologies and laughter on their lips. Glory instantly liked George and Beth Bellows. After introductions, George said, "I've followed your career, Glory. You're one of our best."

"Thanks, George."

"Ever thought about taking up politics?" he asked. "Lady prime ministers is in vogue these days." They all laughed politely. "I'm just the man to get you started."

Edoardo interrupted with. "Hey, George, back off," he growled. "She works with me."

George fell back against the chair, a wide grin spread over his face. "And you don't want to lose the best lawyer you've ever had."

"Too right, I don't," Edoardo said.

"You've got yourself a lovely girl, Edoardo," George said, raising his glass and tilting it towards Glory. "She's something else."

"Thanks, George," Edoardo said.

She didn't like being treated like the little woman and opened her mouth to tell them so when she caught the wink and nod George gave Edoardo signalling that he approved of the *nice* girl he'd chosen and the smug I-knew-I-could-do-it way Edoardo returned the grin.

So darn sure of himself and so darn handsome he made her toes curl inside her shoes.

"Glory, you must have dinner with us soon," Beth suggested pleasantly.

"Love to," Glory answered and they made plans to have dinner at the Bellows' home in Brighton the following Sunday evening.

The women fell into easy conversation and the night flew by.

Before she knew it they were on their way to her home. Edoardo pulled up outside her apartment. She hesitated, bit her bottom lip, and then said, "Would you care to come in for coffee?"

"Thanks, but no thanks," he said. "I've an extra early start in the morning. Martins case."

"Oh, yes, I remember," she said. "Embezzlement isn't it?"

"Yes." He ran his hand along the back of his neck. "And he's been framed for the crime and I know who did it and I've got proof. Tomorrow I'll drop the bombshell."

"Martins will walk free."

"Oh, yes, and his partner Smithers will hear the clank of steel as they lock him up—"

"And throw away the key," she finished for him.

His hand moved to cup her neck beneath her hairline. Gently, oh so gently, he drew her face towards him. The smell of him was spicy, woodsy. It enveloped her, swirled around her, an aromatic tang that left her breathless.

He smiled and her heart grappled with its moorings, and as she stared into the startling blue of his eyes, her heart jerked and went out of control.

"Kiss me," he whispered.

She closed her eyes, counted to three, drew in a breath and said quickly, "I'd better not." Her voice came out low and husky.

He bent his dark head forward and his nose pressed against hers Eskimo-style. Her heart took up such an irregular beat she wondered if it would ever beat normally again. "Why not?"

"I burn easily."

He laughed. His lips brushed hers. "Kiss me, please," he urged.

Experimentally, she pressed her mouth against his. Was that a small earthquake or maybe the car had exploded? She pulled back, but only as far as his restraining hand allowed her.

"Call that a kiss?" he persuaded.

Weak after the heat of his kiss and totally, utterly in love with him, she murmured, "It's the best I can do."

"Doubt that."

His tongue glided over her lower lip and now her heart raced out of control. A warm tingling sensation flowed through her.

Her mind numbed as his mouth claimed hers. He made a nuzzling movement as he sucked her lower lip. His tongue gently circled inside her mouth.

Goosebumps erupted on her arms. She wound her arms around his neck as the kiss intensified into pure passion. Her body became weightless as if she would float away into the atmosphere and become lost in the stars.

She tightened her arms around his neck, and surrendered to his kiss until nothing in the world existed outside of Edoardo and his mouth pressed hard against her own.

Their kiss held, deepened until, breathless, they broke apart.

He looked as shaken as she. "Now that's what I call a kiss."

She was shocked by her reaction to the kiss. She really had lost control. *Weak fool.* She had to get out of here. She groped for the door handle.

He held her back by gently holding her arm. "See you tomorrow."

All her feelings for him had gone into that kiss.

Her utter need of him.

Her wanting him.

And her undying love for him.

There'd never be a Prince Charming because Edoardo was her Prince Charming.

There simply was no other man for her and she loved him so deeply it hurt to think about it.

He would never return her love, not totally, the way she wanted him to.

So what did all this mean? That she would never marry, never have children?

How sad was that?

"Sure," she mumbled, wishing she never had to face him again.

CHAPTER FOUR

Friday night and Glory was excited. They were to attend a fundraising dinner at the town hall where they would also meet the residing Lord Mayor, his wife, and members of the Melbourne City Council. All pomp and circumstances, she knew, but it'd been so long since she'd gone on a date and she was really looking forward to it.

They were leaving after work because the fundraiser started with cocktails at six. Glory had freshened up and was reasonably presentable. She looked up as Edoardo came into her office.

"Ready?"

"And able."

"Let's go." He held out his arm, she threaded hers through his. *Nice.* As they made their way down the corridor towards the elevators, Glory had the oddest thought that this was how she'd always like it to be. Being Edoardo's girl was, well, wonderful.

She knew she wouldn't see him over the weekend, that there weren't any functions until mid-next-week. So she wouldn't see him again until Monday morning when she returned to the office.

Funny, but that didn't sit well with Glory at all.

*

Glory, by habit and desire was an early riser. By six she was working in her back garden.

She had decided, after going to the ABC Gardening Expo, on a Chinese garden. A friend of Kate's, Chu Lee, a landscape gardener, had designed it for Glory, saying bamboo represented a strong but resilient character. *So characteristic of you,* Kate had added. Pine was used to represent longevity, persistence, tenacity, and dignity. Again Kate interrupted, saying, *definitely the real you, Glory.*

And the lotus symbolised purity. Peonies, wealth and riches.

She loved it and, weather permitting, spent hours in the garden reading or working at the rattan table, keeping up her strength and vitality by drinking her favourite, iced coffee with heaps of vanilla ice cream, until the daylight disappeared and dusk descended.

Not a good cook by any stretch of the imagination, Glory usually sent out for take-away from the local Indian restaurant or whizzed down to the local McDonald's for a double cheeseburger and fries.

And when her conscious pricked her and warned her she needed veggies, she'd buy heaps from the local greengrocer's and steaming them, would mash them all together with a large dollop of butter and plenty of milk. The only way she could get them down her throat.

Of course, there was the occasional dinner at Kate's. Glory looked forward to these dinners with great expectations. Kate was a superb cook and her chilli con carne was to die for.

She stood and, with a slight groan, stretched her aching muscles. Throwing down her small trowel and removing her garden gloves, she left them on top of the table and made her way inside the house.

Last night, the fundraiser had been such fun, Glory had been sorry when it was over. Outside her apartment, he'd kissed her, thanking her profusely for being the perfect partner. Then he kissed her again. Long and hard. Head, along with her heart, was reeling as she staggered her way into her apartment.

At work he displayed a powerful presence, which could never be ignored but being with him constantly was proving overwhelming. She couldn't allow herself to give into his sexual persuasion. His using of, she truly believed, a deceptive romantic approach.

Edoardo simply couldn't help himself where women were concerned.

He played the game of love to the hilt, using his allure and magnetism to ensnare his unsuspecting fly into his web, and once captured, he'd set her free with gentle words and most probably an expensive gift, her head still reeling from the impact.

She may be in love with him but she'd never be fooled by his sweet-talk. She was far too heavy-duty, too single-minded to give way to his persuasive allure.

Her success as a lawyer kept her focussed and hard-headed. It was the one thing in her life she could rely on — other than Kate of course.

She'd wondered if what was happening between Edoardo and her would affect their working relationship. She didn't want to leave the practice under any circumstance as she loved her job so much. It wouldn't happen; they were both far too professional to allow anything to interfere with their commitment to the practice and their clients.

She made a light breakfast of cereal with sliced peaches, out of a tin of course, and a slice of toast which she somehow managed to burn. After scraping the toast, she thinly spread it with Vegemite and drank a large glass of icy cold orange juice. Afterwards, she set about thoroughly cleaning her apartment.

Satisfied, she showered and now dressed in tight blue jeans and a pink Angora turtleneck jumper. She made a cup of coffee and settled down to work on the deposition she needed for Monday's court.

It was a particularly gruelling case where her client had been accused of stealing very important hush-hush data from the large conglomerate she worked for and covertly selling it to their opposition. Glory had Burt Mayebelle, one of their investigators, working on the case. Burt would suss out any and all skulduggery.

She looked up and frowned at the sound of the doorbell. It was probably Kate and Aiden, insisting she come to their house for dinner, that Kate was cooking cheesy meatballs with spaghetti, followed by apple pie and vanilla ice-cream, Glory's favourite meal, knowing Glory couldn't resist even though she'd planned a quiet evening at home.

Tossing down the pen, she made her way to the front door thinking Kate would most probably lure her by hiring a film or two. *Dear John,* she'd been busting to see, or her all-time favourite from the 1940s *Her Girl Friday* with Rosalind Russell and Cary Grant. She loved that movie. Okay, so she was a sucker for romance. She had to get her kicks from somewhere, didn't she?

Glory swung open the door. And he stood there, with his wicked smile and flashing bad-boy eyes. It suddenly occurred to her that he was the image of Cary Grant, a combination of virility, sexuality, and the aura and bearing of a gentleman.

Dressed in a long-sleeved white polo shirt and blue jeans, which were moulded to his body as if he'd been poured into them and someone had forgotten to say whoa. He wore loafers without socks.

His cologne smelled great, like vanilla beans. Glory liked it.

Her eyes fluttered, tried to ignore the hot flush spreading itself, with impish delight, throughout her body.

"Hi."

She folded her arms. "I didn't know you were coming. What are you doing here?" She didn't mean to sound so snappy. Why did he bring out the worst in her? Why was she always so darn defensive? And why in the hell was he here in the first place?

He drew back from her, his hands held up as if he were under house arrest. "Hey," he murmured, his blue eyes twinkling roguishly, "is that any way to treat your boyfriend?"

She grinned. He was so hard to resist. "Oh, darn, come on in. I'll put on a pot of fresh coffee."

"Where's your house keys?"

"On that table." She jerked her head towards a small hall table standing near the front door. He reached around and grabbed the keys, shoving them inside his jeans pocket. Then quite slowly and intentionally, he drew her into him. "Come out and play."

Startled, she offered no resistance but her eyes grew wide and her breath caught in her throat as her breasts pressed flat against his solid chest.

For one heady moment she knew he'd kiss her and she braced herself for the full impact. Half of her desperate for his kiss, the other half warning her of the staggering impact it would have on her emotions.

She was in for vast disappointment as Edoardo didn't kiss her, but almost carried her to the elevator. "Where are we going?" she managed to say.

"For a long drive." He pressed the down button. "Just you, me, and the birdies in the trees."

Ignoring the surge of excitement at being alone with him, she tucked her hand into her hip. "And so I have to go?" She looked around, feigning doubtfulness. "Can't see any reporters. Can't see any members of council. Is George in the car with a tape recorder and video camera to record a day of fun and laughter with Glory and Edoardo?"

"Now, Glory that's not nice," he said, sounding not the least disconcerted by her outburst. "You'll enjoy a day in the country, away from the city smells, to relax and not do a thing but have fun."

He took a step towering over her. "You say I work you too hard, and you moan and groan when we have to attend an official function, so I thought, why not give her a special treat. Show her I'm not the workhorse she thinks I am."

She drew herself to her full height. "I do not moan and groan. I simply state the situation as it is."

His left eyebrow raised a fraction. "Or as you see it, maybe."

"Don't twist my words, Edoardo," she said. "You're not in court."

She could control any situation, even a fire alarm situation, by calmly, with her co-workers in tow, leave the building. She could deal with an earthquake by yelling out "everyone under your desk," but in this instance she was way out of her depth.

She glanced down at what she was wearing. Oh my God, she was dressed for a backyard barbeque. And worse still, she was without a repair kit. He hadn't given her time to grab her handbag with her compact and lipstick.

"Couldn't you have let me change?"

His gaze travelled up and down her body. "You look great."

Breathless, she followed him out of the elevator, through the tiny foyer that was more an entrance walk than anything else, and into his waiting car.

He had a different car. A Bufori Madison, a car that embodied the style and class of the 1930s roadster, coupled with the state-of-the-art technology.

"Do you want the top down?"

"That'd be great." She glanced at the sky, and although the wind softly moaned, it was a milk-and-honey day, a day to be with someone you loved, a day to be young and carefree and forget about the whys and wherefores or the whether she should or shouldn't codes of life.

Yes, she'd make today hers, and not allow a thing to spoil it. Not even the fact that Edoardo would never love her. She understood the situation, accepted it with as much dignity as she could muster, and went along with it.

He tossed a baseball cap into her lap. "Tuck your hair into this. Otherwise it'll blow all over your face." She did as he asked. "You look cute."

She rolled her eyes. "Cute?" she echoed, bowled over. "Me? I look cute. Ever considered contact lenses?" She laughed softly.

He looked right into her eyes, kept his gaze steady and even. He gave a tongue-in-cheek smile. "Anything wrong with being cute?"

She merely arched a brow at him although her heart skipped a beat at his backhanded compliment. "Babies are cute, puppies are cute, and tiny little kittens are really cute—"

The engine roared into life. "I like babies, puppies, and kittens," he said. He threw the car into gear and took off. "And I like you."

Oh, she didn't doubt for a moment that he liked her, respected her as his colleague, but that was so ordinary. She wanted him to sit up and take notice. Drool from the corners of his mouth every time she came into view. She wanted all other women to fade into insignificance when she was with him.

She wanted him to fall desperately, madly in love with her.

She glanced over at him. His hair ruffled by the wind, his blue eyes glittery, almost iniquitous.

She'd liked what he'd said about her being cute, and he really was sweet and she found him hard to resist. He radiated some kind of light. Okay, his nose bridge had a bump as if he'd been in a fist fight or two but that added rather than subtracted.

He was, to put it meekly, a sex rocket ready and set to fire you to the moon. Question remained, would he bring her back?

She nestled back into the soft leather of the car. She relaxed. A trip to the country was just what she needed.

She couldn't remember when she'd been out of the city. Always too busy with arranging suitable court dates, interviewing clients, taking dispositions, she'd almost forgotten there was solitude and nature not that far from the CBD.

Although again, she couldn't help wondering why he was taking her on an unofficial date? Did Edoardo have an ulterior motive? Although she couldn't imagine what he'd want from her that he couldn't ask outright. Hmm, had this outing somehow been George's idea? And if so, why? If not, why did Edoardo want to spend time with her when he certainly didn't have to?

Darn, why did it matter one way or the other? This was extremely strange but totally divine.

Until this moment everything had been so bureaucratic. George had arranged a dinner party, or a press conference, or cocktails with a visiting VIP. Always someone with them, never alone, never tempted, which, she reassured herself, was exactly how she wanted it to be.

"Not too cold?" he yelled. "I've got a jacket in the back."

She was freezing. The wind whistled around her, plucked at her clothing as if seeking entrance. "No, I don't need a jacket. I love it," she cried, and he pressed the accelerator down.

*

Edoardo didn't know what made him call by her apartment. He was just idly driving around, deciding where to go, what to do, when wham there he was outside her place.

He had sat outside in the street for ages before he'd got the nerve to knock on her door. Why he should worry about calling on her baffled him even more. Hell, they had worked together now for over two years and he'd always been comfortable in her company.

How much he enjoyed staying back with her at the practice, discussing and arguing how to handle a difficult case, sending out for take-away, and drinking hot chocolate out of paper cups.

And yet now …

He had nothing planned, no ulterior motive about seeing her, or even what he'd say to her. It had been an impulse he'd found difficult to resist, and not being a man to hold back on his urges, he'd simply gone with the flow.

He couldn't get this woman out of his head, right from the first moment he'd asked her to be his girlfriend. Well, before that actually. There was something about Glory. The magnificence of her hair, the beauty of her eyes and the way her pretty face lit up when she smiled.

Most women were bowled over when he spread on the charm, but not Glory Sandrin, and it seemed to him that no matter what he did, or how hard he tried, he simply couldn't please her.

One minute he had her worked out and the next she confounded him until his head swirled.

His hands gripped the steering wheel. She was the type of woman he could become a fool over and he didn't like it.

So why did he carry this desperate need for her? It made no sense.

After all, he was dating this gorgeous fashion model. Bunny didn't spin his mind out of control. She didn't argue with every single word he uttered and was happy, content even, to see him and no strings attached.

Maybe he should call on Bunny. Maybe that's what this was all about. Forget all about a little girl who could twist his emotions around her little finger, and send his temperature soaring at the blink of her lashes.

All he needed was a night with Bunny and everything would come up smelling like roses.

So why he didn't go to Bunny's apartment was far beyond him.

Yet somehow, and call this stupid because it was beyond dim-witted, it was as if he were cheating on Glory, even thinking about another woman. How preposterous was that?

He took a quick glance at her.

He'd been burned and the scars still throbbed.

He'd never take a chance on love again.

He could act out this little charade no problem and, when it was over, no regrets.

They left the sounds of the city far behind them. He took the Princes Highway and for the next couple of hours or so they drove in relative silence except every now and then Glory broke into a song when the radio played one of her favourites.

He didn't know any other woman who had sung to him when

they were in the car. Glory was so natural, the girl next door, the girl you'd grown up with.

He slowed down at Terang and did a sharp right turn.

"Where are we going?"

"Noorat."

She furrowed her brow, concentrating on the name. "Never heard of it."

He flashed a frown. "Come on, Glory. Noorat. Alan Marshall. The man who wrote, *I Can Jump Puddles*—"

"Story teller and social documenter," she cried excitedly. "I read his entire three-book autobiography. When he was six years old he contracted polio leaving him with a physical disability that grew worse as he grew older."

"See, you do know about him. Marshall was born in a shop, which is still a mixed business. Dalvui homestead," he said. "I believe the gardens are magnificent. Designed by William Guilfoyle, who designed the Botanical Gardens."

"William who?"

"Guilfoyle." He sighed — loudly. "In 1873 he became director and changed the style of the Gardens by adding tropical plants."

She gasped loudly. "You're unbelievable. How do you know all this?"

He chuckled. "I've read extensively on the state of Victoria."

*

Glory laughed softly, amazed at him and how he surprised her every time she was with him. "Let me hang my head in shame," she said. "I'd be lucky if I could recite the main streets of the city."

His lips twitched with amusement. "Don't be. Most people don't know enough about their home states." His mouth broadened into a grin. "I was showing off."

Like a schoolboy trying to impress his teacher, and her heart warmed to him. "Were you? Showing off, I mean?"

"Yes."

A thrill raced through her. "Why?"

She liked his thick hair tapering neatly to his collar; the contrast against the stark white of his shirt startling. "To impress you."

It excited her knowing he wanted to please her. "Well, you succeeded."

He pulled over to the side of the road and braked. She sat upright. "What is it?"

"A fair?"

She looked around. "What?"

He pointed. "A county fair. I haven't been to a fair since I was in knee pants." He opened the car door and got out. "Come on," he said, and she hastened to oblige because he was halfway across the highway as it was.

Glory threw a quick look left and right. She had to run to catch up with him.

They followed the metallic music of the carousel and the bright lights of the fairgrounds.

As they entered the fairgrounds, he took her hand and they walked together, like — well, if not like lovers at least friends.

She couldn't remember ever coming to a country fair. She supposed she must have in her youth, but the memory escaped her.

She glanced around at the screams from the riders of the Ferris wheel and the barkers enticing you to 'ave-a-go and win a celluloid doll or a stuffed toy or enter the sideshows to see the bearded lady, the half-man half-woman, or the man with two heads.

A pulse of excitement came from being in this different world, a world of holiday-time and utter pleasure, forgetting about law books and statements and court calendars and just being young and free and living life to the full.

A kiosk sold crispy cones of ice cream and sugar floss spun onto sticks and twisted into crazy twirls of candy pink and a memory of its taste stung her tongue and she recalled a time at the Melbourne Royal Show with her parents, when she had been around six or seven. How excited she had been to see the carousal and begged to be allowed to ride it three or four times.

She remembered now how her father had enclosed her mother to him, his large arm wrapped around her shoulders, squeezing her affectionately, and when Glory had complained of being tired how he had swept her up high upon his shoulders.

She had loved her dad desperately, almost a hero worship, and he had left her alone with her mum who, bewildered by the loss of the only man she had ever loved, had faded away like an old photograph.

She glanced at Edoardo. He was the same type of man as her father. He was a man who enjoyed life to the hilt, a man who went after what he wanted, a man who had no compunction to love and leave, without consequence, the same as Kate's husband, Greg. He'd just dumped his wife and child like they meant nothing to him. Poor Kate, alone now with a broken heart and memories of a man who loved another woman more than his wife.

Edoardo was a man who loved all women, and who would never give his heart to just one woman.

A man so not for her.

She pushed away the feeling of wretchedness that threatened to overcome her. *Snap out of it. Not now, not today.* Today was meant for happiness and she intended to enjoy every moment of it.

They came to a shooting gallery and Edoardo tried his luck. He missed the target frequently.

"Weren't you ever in the army cadets?" She gave his arm a tug. "Give me a go."

He looked down at her. "Good God, why?"

"I may do better."

"Yes, and you may do murder," he shot back.

She reached for the rifle. "Give it to me," she insisted.

Edoardo blew out a breath. "Back off," he said, raising the rifle out of her reach. He leaned over the counter, tucked the rifle butt into his shoulder, and took careful, deliberate aim. He missed. "Damn thing," he muttered. "The sights must be off."

"Your sight is off. Let me show you how it's done."

"Okay, smarty-pants, go for broke." He handed her the rifle. "Show me how it's done." He crossed his arms across his massive chest, glaring down at her, challenging her. She took up the challenge eagerly.

She leaned over the counter, aimed and fired, managing to win a rather odd-shaped teddy bear. She handed the rifle to the man behind the counter and the teddy bear to Edoardo. "Annie Oakley has nothing on me." She gave him a told-you-so grin.

He chuckled, and then laughed loudly and when he spoke, his voice was filled with admiration. "Now I'm totally impressed. You're in the wrong profession, Glory; you should've joined the police force."

"Hmm, I did consider that at one time. *G.I. Jane* with Demi Moore in camouflage and toting a rifle over one shoulder decided the army was for me."

"What made you change your mind?"

"All that marching. I've got delicate feet."

His laughter. His smiling eyes. "How did you learn to shoot so well?"

"My dad took me rifle range shooting when I was a kid," she explained.

He handed the teddy-bear to a small child in a pusher. The mother smiled her thanks. "Want to go on the roller coaster?"

He looked different, younger, if possible more handsome, and she was different too, light-hearted and joyful, as if she were expecting something wonderful to happen. "I'm game if you are."

He took her hand and they crossed the fairgrounds to the roller coaster. She'd never been on a roller coaster, wasn't a person who liked scary rides, and her heart looped in her chest.

He insisted they sit in the front seat although she pleaded with him to sit in the middle seat. "Chicken," he said and at his dare, she huddled miserably, into the seat beside him.

It was terrifying; it was horrendous, it was breathtaking — Glory, now devoid of thought as to what she should or shouldn't do, wrapped herself around him and burying herself into his bulk, screamed at every dip and turn.

"Want to go again?" he asked her, rather out of breath himself.

She was out of the car before she answered him, her legs quivering like jelly and her head spinning like a toy top. "If I ever get the urge to go on a roller coaster again," she said drily, "please take me to the nearest analyst."

His eyes glinted with tomfoolery. "Where's your sense of adventure? For an Annie Oakley, you sure crack under pressure."

"Undue pressure." She gave him, what she hoped was a quelling look. "And my adventurous spirit vanished somewhere between the death loop and the loop of perpetual terror."

He laughed and threaded her arm through his leading her away from the roller coaster. "Feeling any better?" Edoardo's gaze didn't shift from her face. "You're face is still washed-out."

"Washed-out," she exclaimed. "Couldn't you have found a nicer word?"

He feigned concentration. "There's sickly or colourless. Hmm, maybe it's a light green."

Tilting her head back, she peered at his face. "I'll stick with washed-out, thanks."

His fingers were warm and strong as he grasped hers. "Are you really okay?"

She promptly disengaged her hands. Warm and wonderful, she said, "Yes, my hair's stopped standing on end."

He laughed again and she suffered a sense of extreme excitement. Almost as if she knew something amazing was going to happen between them — but that was only her vivid imagination, her desperate hope that Edoardo would change and love her the way she loved him. Give her what she so wanted with him, a home and babies.

Master Plan, Master Plan, she reminded herself. *I will meet Prince Charming, and he will whisk me off on his white steed to a home in the suburbs where, contented just to be together, we'll have heaps of kids, a mangy old dog and a cat or two.* She must never stray from the Master Plan.

She glanced at him. What about sex with this incomparable half of the dynamic duo? Could she go to bed with him and come out not panting for more? Maybe, maybe not. Was she resilient enough to have a brief affair, tip her hat and say, *wham-bang-thank-you-man*?

"Okay, let's see what else is offering," he said as they moved further into the fair grounds. "What's over there? Hmmm, Madame Zelare's. Want your fortune told?"

"It could be fun. Although I don't believe anyone can foretell the future. It's pure playacting."

"What do you believe?"

"That the future is in your own hands." She folded her arms and nodded slowly. "You can change it if you want to. Like if you come to a crossroads and you're unsure which way to take. The decision must be to take the safest route, the one that will bring you out to where you want to be."

He shook his head slightly. "You make it sound all so uncomplicated." He cocked his head to one side. "I never knew you were such a realist."

She shrugged. "I try to keep my feet firmly on the ground at all times."

"So you don't take chances?"

She raised an eyebrow. "Like on what?"

His eyes grew dark. "I don't know; cards maybe or the lottery, or crossing the road against the lights." He gazed down at her. "Or love."

Her heart took up such an irregular beat and she briefly closed her eyes. "Do you take chances, Edoardo? Would you take a chance on love?"

"Typical lawyer tactics; answer a question with a question." He gave her a tiny push. "In you go then," he said shoving money into her hand and ushering her gently towards the large tent. "I'll wait out here for you."

"But—" she protested.

"And don't start in with cross-examining the poor woman. This is purely for fun only." He reached out to lightly touch her cheek. "Go on," he urged her, and half-heartedly, she entered the tent.

It was dark almost pitch black and Glory blinked her eyes, adjusting to the gloomy light. She turned around at the rustle of curtain beads and a tall, extremely thin woman appeared.

Her hair was long and stringy and jet-black, and she was dressed flamboyantly in swirling colours of purple, aquamarine, yellow, and green. Large silver hoop earrings adorned her earlobes and she was swathed in strings of multicoloured beads. Kate would kill for this outfit.

She took a seat and bid Glory to do the same. "You wish the tarot cards or palm reading?"

Oddly nervous, Glory said the first thing that came into her head. "I wish the palm reading. Thanks very much."

Madame Zelare took Glory's hand in her own, running a fingertip lightly across her palm. Glory trembled. "You are unhappy? You love but are not loved?"

Glory nodded, rather amazed at the fortune-teller's ability to get to the truth so quickly. Maybe she was too hasty in her judgment and, as Edoardo put it, too down-to-earth.

Madame Zelare smiled benevolently. "Unhappiness and happiness are interlocked, my dear, one cannot be without the other. Like day and night. Right and wrong. Love and hate," she chanted as if she'd said the same thing a hundred times before.

Glory looked away from the fortune teller and inclined her face towards the slim strip of bright sunlight streaming through the tent opening. "I don't understand. I'm not sure what you mean."

"You will understand in time," she intoned. "Follow your heart."

Follow my heart? Dear God, if I did that where in the heck would I be? The only thing I'll follow is my logic, and that's telling me to keep my cool.

Glory was glad to be out in the bright sunlight, breathing the fresh air.

"How did it go?"

She shrugged. "All right, I guess. The usual prattle of a seasoned fortune-teller. It was an experience, if nothing else."

He reached out to touch her hair. And, strangely unsettled, she moved back from his touch. "Anything you want to share with me?"

She shook her head slightly. "Nothing. It was textbook stuff."

He laughed softly. "Did she say you'd meet a tall, dark handsome stranger?"

Glory's eyes met Edoardo's. "She said, beware of strangers. Only trust people you know."

His eyes were dark, dangerous. "Like me?"

"Yes," she whispered. She took a deep breath letting it out slowly. "Like you."

It wasn't what they were saying, it was the way they said it. Her heart was beating way too fast.

A newborn wind stirred the restless trees, and blew dry leaves along the path upon which they were walking. The sun chose to play hide and seek with a cloud yet still the day was magic.

In the distance she could hear the shrill crassak-crassak of a king parrot in flight and a kookaburra laughing as though he'd heard the joke of the century. Was the joke on her?

They went into the fun house and she squealed when the floor beneath them came to life and turned into a revolving disc. He grabbed her hand as they managed to scramble onto solid wood.

Pushing through a rubber-stripped arch, they tumbled into a pitch-black tunnel. She grabbed his hand. He squeezed hers. If he kissed her, here in the darkness, utterly alone and so darn vulnerable, goodness knows what would happen between them.

She knew she'd kiss him back with all the pent-up emotions she had inside her. Dangerous ground. "Don't even think about it," she said.

She heard his chuckle. How much he was enjoying flirting with her with any woman that took his fancy. "Spoiled sport."

"Just find me light."

He tugged her though a slit of light into the hall of mirrors. She wandered away from him, but he grabbed her hand and dragged her back. "Look," he said. The warped reflection showed two very rotund figures. "This is how we'll look when we're sixty."

Sixty? They would be lucky to get through the mayoral campaign.

He moved her along. Their reflections were like beanpoles now. He made a face and she giggled. "You look like Stan Laurel. Another fine mess you've got me into, Stanley," she mimicked.

He quickly looked down at her. His eyes a deep blue mist. "Have I?"

She swallowed harshly. "What?"

He gathered her close so that the side of her head pressed against his chest, his hand held firmly against her upper arm. She couldn't have escaped from him had she wanted to. "Got you into a mess."

His hold loosened and she wriggled out of his embrace, hesitated, and then said, "I'm used to messes."

His brow was furrowed in concern. "Something you want to tell me?"

She shrugged and moved away from him. "After my father left, my mother fretted her life away," she explained, wanting now to tell him about her parents, her life as a child. "She barely came out of her bedroom. She ate like a bird and she hardly talked at all. It was as if she'd taken a vow to punish herself for what my dad had done to her. As if it were her fault he'd left. I couldn't do much to help her except care for her, be there for her."

"Sounds tough going for both of you."

"My teenage years were erratic and unpredictable. Made me strongly independent and more than a little crazy too, I think."

He gave her a careful look. "Your mother couldn't take her husband leaving her? Couldn't get her life together?"

"She lost interest in everything. I had to take over the reins. Sometimes she didn't know I was there. It was awful for her. Me too I guess."

"How old were you?"

"Fifteen."

At her words, he went still. "My God, so young, and yet you managed to get through university and law school and pass with honours." He paused, his blue eyes intense. "I knew you were special. How did you do it?"

"It's the English in me," she said sheepishly. "Makes me determined to achieve the unachievable." She laughed a little self-consciously. "Actually, the truth was I had no other alternative."

He looked down at her and smiled a contemplative little ghost of a smile. "No other relatives? Grandparents? An aunt maybe?"

"Just Mum and me."

He arched a brow at her. "Has it made you anti-marriage?"

"Hey, I wouldn't go that far," she said backing off, raising her palm in a placatory gesture. "With the right man—?"

"The settling down type of man? A man that offers marriage, the works?"

I want you, if only you were different. "I'll find him one day."

"Yes, I guess you will." His voice was tinged with melancholy as if he regretted something he'd done or hadn't yet done. "And you deserve nothing but the best, Glory." He hesitated, and then added, "And I hope you find this Prince Charming of yours. He's a lucky bloke."

Glory blew out a breath before saying, "I believe in the—"

"The institution of marriage?" he cut in.

"Who wants to live in an institution," they both chorused and laughed gleefully.

He reached out and took her hand, walking with her from the fun house outside into the crisp air. The sun had disappeared and dark clouds gathered. Still the day was magic. Edoardo placed his arm around her shoulders, drawing her closer to him. Now *that* she liked. It seemed so natural and warm and totally safe.

"Are you getting cold feet?" he asked her. "About pretending to be my girl?"

"My feet are wrapped in ice."

He raked a hand back through his hair and exhaled. "It's only for a short time."

"What if I blow it?"

"How can you do that?" he asked, seeming genuinely stunned by her answer.

"Oh, right, all I have to do is act the loving girlfriend." *I can do that. Anyone can do that.* A fine chill threaded through her, sending icy fingers up and down her spine. *Can't I? Oh God, can't I?*

"Hey, Glory, look on it like an adventure," he said with a ghost of a chuckle. "We can laugh our legs off once I get into office. A grand story to tell your grandchildren," he ended.

She stared at Edoardo, disappointment humming inside like a bumble-bee. She'd known what was in store, that he'd viewed the whole deal as a game, and when it was over, he'd have a big chuckle about it all, and expect her to respond in kind.

Still, she'd made a deal with him ... "It means that much to you?"

"Yes, it does."

"Then no worries," she said. "I made a deal and intend keeping to it."

He stopped walking and stood directly in front of her. "So I guess we're stuck with each other."

Heat flared in his blue eyes, hot and dangerous. "I guess," she muttered.

He stared over her shoulder and she turned to see what he was looking at. The sign read, *The original and only Love Boat — the most romantic trip in the world.* He raised an eyebrow. "My treat."

Her head jerked back involuntarily. "No way. You're not getting me in that."

He studied her shrewdly. She shifted her feet restlessly. "Why not?"

Why not? Because she couldn't bear being alone in the dark with him, knowing he would touch her, knowing he would kiss her, knowing he would think it all some crazy, wonderful game, a game where he made up the rules.

A game of love where there was no chance for her to ever win.

She shrugged carelessly although her stomach churned. "I get seasick at the idea of boats."

A few drops of rain splattered them. They glanced up. Storm clouds were rolling in. He moved in dangerously close. His eyes were so blue. Clear, open eyes. Wonderful eyes. Eyes she could stare into forever.

"You know what I think?"

"No, what do you think?"

"That you're scared of me."

"Me? Scared of you?" She gave a contemptuous chuckle, sounding very much like an evil goblin at the end of the garden. "You're joking, of course," she threw the remark away carelessly.

He remained quiet, studying her as intently as a prisoner in the dock; waiting for the right moment to strike out with the winning piece of evidence that would close the case. "Hmmm, I wonder." Then he said, "Hungry?"

For you. "Starving."

"How about a hamburger, chips, and a Coke?" he suggested. "I noticed there was a small cafe near the entrance to the grounds."

"Sounds a plan."

They passed an open field and a single wild Pink Fingers orchid fluttered in the cool breeze. A lush fringe of pale pink petals spread outward from the orchid's dark centre. He leaned over a small wire fence and plucked the flower from the earth.

"To match your cheeks," he said as he handed it to her.

Heart meltdown time. She brought the bloom to her nose and inhaled deeply. "Thanks."

As she walked beside Edoardo, the wind flowed over her skin like the soft touch of velvet. She could hear the delicate orchestra of bird sounds, the rustling of leaves and the trees swaying, whispering some magical secret to each other.

They reached the open-sided cafe, the top covered with a canvas awning, and sat at a small wooden table with their food. She picked up the saltcellar and freely sprinkled her chips. He leaned towards her and she drew back.

"What are you doing?" she demanded, her heart pounding in her chest like a blacksmith's mallet.

His fingers grazed her chin. "You have salt on your chin." His gaze deepened as he licked the salt from his finger. Her breath caught in her throat.

To ease her thudding heart, she said easily, "Did I spill any?"

Edoardo drew back. "Surely you're not superstitious?" he said.

She pressed her lips together. "I guess I am a little superstitious."

"Spilling salt is more of a legend," he pronounced. "Salt is used in the preparation of holy water and it wasn't uncommon to put salt into a coffin."

"What! What did you say?" she paused with her mouth open and stared at him. "A coffin!"

He laughed at her knocked for six expression. "Satan hates salt."

"Is this for real?" He nodded and she laughed delightedly. "How do you know about this salt business?"

"No mystery. I did research on ancient legends for a paper I was preparing for uni."

"You're terrific." The words tumbled from her mouth. "Do you know that?"

He grinned. "If you say so, makes me humbly agree."

"You're staring at me," she said. He left her breathless. She was on a high as if she'd drunk too much champagne. She wanted him with the same feeling as wanting air.

"Am I?" His lips curled up. "Sorry."

A strong, almost dangerous, response that left her feeling vulnerable and slightly afraid overcame her. "You like what you see?" she challenged.

"Very much so."

She wanted to answer that she liked him too but her pride held the words back.

"Maybe a mutual admiration society?" he said with a soft chuckle.

"No comment on that, me lud." A moment of silence followed.

He leaned over the table, right in Glory's face and said casually, "Pretty soon, you'll have to meet my parents."

She pulled back as far as her chair allowed. Was he kidding? Meet the parents? No way. She'd met enough of his contemporaries, friends, and strangers even, to last a lifetime. Parents, to put it frantically, were way off her to-visit list.

"Why must I meet your parents? Surely it's not necessary," she said. "After all, Edoardo, I'm the girlfriend and that's for a short time only." Her defence system took control. "I'm positive you don't take all your girlfriends home to meet your parents; your mother would have to have a limitless supply of coffee and cake — besides which it would surely confuse them."

"I've never taken a girl home to meet my parents."

Contrite, she said, "Then why me?"

He looked away from her from a moment, before returning his gaze and saying, "She saw a photo of us in a magazine, and she's upset that I haven't brought you to meet her." He laughed but it wasn't a laugh of mirth. "Be warned, she wants me married." Then hastily added. "Don't worry, that's a plunge I'll never do again."

Married? My God, she'd had no idea. "I didn't know you'd been married," she said in a low soft voice.

"Long story. It was years ago."

"Do you want to talk about it?"

He hesitated then said, "Sophia was the daughter of my mother's best friend. We grew up together; went to the same school. I took her to the school dance. First kiss." He ran his fingers over the stubble on his chin. "You know the way it works.

"They threw us together at every opportunity. I was young, just twenty, and before I knew what was happening I was walking down the aisle."

He threw back his head and studied the blue-and-white striped awning. Connecting his eyes to hers, he said, "She was obsessive in her love for me. Telephoning all hours of the day, even when she knew I was in court. Questioning me — or should I say giving me the third degree. And then the false accusations began. I was with another woman. I didn't love her anymore. I stuck it for as long as I could then I left."

He had her full attention now. "She threatened suicide. Took to stalking me. Waiting outside my apartment. Turning up at work at the most inopportune times." He gave a slight shudder.

"That's so awful," she said, genuinely upset for him. "For both of you."

"Yes, it was. Funny thing is, I believed in marriage," he said. "The idea of one man and one woman making a life together, having children and a house in the burbs appealed to me."

My sentiments exactly. "And now marriage has lost its appeal?"

"For years I kept my cool, trying to make a success of our marriage, until my nerves snapped and the heated arguments began. My life became unbearable and I knew Sophia's life wasn't fairing much better.

"So for both our sakes, I walked out and filed for divorce. The only thing that kept me sane was work, and I threw myself into that, working twelve, sometimes fourteen hours a day."

She longed to reach over and touch him and comfort him. What right did she have to touch him? She didn't belong to Edoardo. She was a surrogate woman in his private life. Someone he didn't make promises to, apologies to.

A woman he didn't have to love.

She'd always wondered why he was so shy of commitment. Now she knew — and who could blame him? He'd been burned and the scars still throbbed. He'd never take a chance like that again.

Glory's heart ached for him and for her as well. Before she had a hope that he'd get tired of playing the field, but now there was no hope. Maybe in a strange weird way it was for the best, because now she'd simply concentrate on her Master Plan. Her love for him would settle somewhere deep inside her; and as years passed and she sat with her children by the fire, she'd remember and wonder ...

He gave a slight shake to his head as if to rid it of old demons.

"Trust me, I'll never put myself though that hell again," he said. His eyes went a misty blue, fascinating Glory by the intensity of their colour. "Never."

Ignoring the pain in her heart, she said, "What happened to Sophia?"

"After around a year or so, she met someone else, a farmer from New Zealand. They married and she went with him to Auckland."

"Is she happy now?"

He grinned. "Trust you to ask that question. According to my mother, yes, she's happy. Ron, that's her husband, is with her 24/7 and that's what she's always wanted."

"Not all women are like your ex."

He looked at her. That was all he did, looked at her, and love rushed through her like spring rain. "I don't like that aspect of love," he said softly. "I don't like the controlling part of love."

"Sometimes things get way out of our control," she said.

"I like being in control. Control is good."

"Me too."

He hesitated, his brow furrowing. He looked at her so oddly, as if he were about to say something important and deciding against it.

His laugh was light, almost gay. "Hey, I've talked up a storm."

And then he leaned over the table and kissed her lightly on the mouth. The very moment his lips met hers Glory lost the power to think. A deep yearning and a bottomless hunger for him overcame her.

"Want I should get you coffee?" he murmured against her lips.

"No."

"Want a glass of milk?"

Heart thudding erratically in her chest, she shook her head.

A devilish look came into his eyes. "Want to go to bed with me?"

She quickly pulled her head back from his dynamic mouth. "What? What did you say?"

The smouldering brilliance of his eyes sent a flash of desire through her. "Can't blame a man for trying." His chuckle was deep and warm. "I'm having another Coke. Can I get you anything from the counter?"

She needed something to bring down her rapidly rising temperature. "I'd like an ice cream cone. A double-header. Vanilla. And in a crispy cone, not a cup." Her voice was passionless, though her pulse hurdled like a sprinter in a race.

Glory studied Edoardo's broad strong back as he walked to the counter, the way he stood, self-esteem and a touch of arrogance in his stride.

He'd made it totally clear that he would never marry again, and that was all she ever wanted.

A home and a family with her own Prince Charming.

CHAPTER FIVE

Glory had arranged to meet Kate for lunch at the Cherry Blossom Cafe, a familiar place, a comfortable place where they had spent many a lunch hour lamenting the woes of working in a law practice.

The cafe was located down a cobblestone side street at the top end of North Bourne Avenue. Yawning branches of a flowering cherry blossom stretched like a languid cat across the windows of the cafe.

Glory was the first to arrive. Choosing a table nearest the window, she ordered their lunch. Gazing down the street her eyes searched for Kate.

Kate walked as if she hadn't a care in the world. Her hands dug deep into the pockets of her cropped coat. Her hair a glorious bright red, braided into two stiff plaits sticking out the side of her head like candy canes. Glory could tell, even from this distance, that Kate was whistling. She was such a sweet, familiar sight that Glory experienced a ray of comfort.

She gave Kate a small wave as she threaded her way around the tables to sit opposite her. "G'day," she said brightly. "You look exhausted. You've got dark circles under the eyeballs."

"Gee, thanks, Kate, I was feeling great till you came and put me straight."

Kate studied her intently. "You've been dodging me. Why so?"

"I haven't."

"Glory, we haven't spoken in depth for donks." Again she scrutinized her face. "And I repeat, why?"

A prickly retort sprang to her lips. Glory swallowed it. "If this is how you address your friends, Kate, you should consider reading

How to Win Friends and Influence People in great depth."

Kate grinned widely, like the Cheshire cat out of *Alice in Wonderland*. "I consider edging up to things or sneaking through the back door, a complete and utter waste of time and energy."

"Don't I know it."

Glory signalled for the waitress who immediately came and placed a platter of mixed sandwiches onto the table. "I got us some sandwiches," she said, stating the obvious.

Kate reached for her purse. "Great," she said. "How much do I owe?"

"My treat."

"About time," she grouched. "You owe me for three lunches already."

Glory straightened up in her chair. "Ever heard of thanks."

"Thanks." Kate looked around. "Did you order some coffee?"

Glory nodded.

Choosing a cheese and green-pickle sandwich Kate took a generous bite. Munching, she mumbled, "This affair is a bit sudden, don't cha think?"

Glory frowned. "You've got to stop this annoying habit, Kate."

"What habit would that be, Glory?" she asked with phony innocence.

"Of coming directly to the point. It's like being hit in the face with a sledge-hammer." She nibbled, half-heartedly on a tomato and lettuce sandwich.

"Sorry," Kate murmured, both knowing that she wasn't the least bit sorry, nor did she intend changing lifelong habits. "Do you really like him, Glory? I mean what's going on here?"

"Hey, what's this — the third degree? I'm just having some fun and so is Edoardo. Okay?"

Kate chose another sandwich and looked into Glory's eyes. She resisted the temptation to lower hers. If she couldn't hold Kate's gaze, Kate would put two and two together and come up with five.

Glory didn't dare breathe a word of the subterfuge. The press, if they found out, it would kill Edoardo's chances of becoming Mayor. Yet she hated keeping secrets from Kate. How would it look in her friend's eyes if she said, *Kate, this is a sham relationship. He doesn't love me and never will. It's a sort of bargain, that's all. I'm helping him gain mayoral office, and he's — he's … a rat fink.*

Kate straightened her back. "Look, I've known you long enough to give me the right to say exactly what I think. We talk about everything, you and me. There's nothing I don't know about you and vice versa, and all of a sudden, without as such as a how-do-you-do you clam up tighter than a miser's purse."

Glory reached over and touched her hand. "I don't mean to hurt you. That's the last thing I had in mind," she said. "Why I'd rather put my head into a meat grinder than hurt you."

Kate grinned. "Can I watch?"

Glory chuckled. "You'd faint. You know you can't stand the sight of blood."

"Just tell me how the affair began. I mean, did he come on to you, or did you come on to him? I'd put money on the latter."

To tell Kate the truth was impossible, and she didn't want to lie to her friend. She never had and she never would. Not big lies anyway. Not the lies that make people mistrust you. Little lies were okay, they were usually said to protect someone's feeling.

Like when Kate asked how did she like her latest hairstyle or colour, and, even though it looked like Kate had been in a wind-tunnel and her hair sparkled like sequins on a clown costume, Glory would say it was great.

But this time if she told Kate that she'd insisted Edoardo pay Kate the bonus, Kate would immediately give the money back to Edoardo and quit her job.

She couldn't allow that to happen. No way. She wanted her friend out of harm's way and protected as much as was within her power. Kate had enough on her plate being a single mum to a boisterous four-year-old.

"I couldn't fight the urge." She shrugged. "Don't worry. It's nothing serious. Not for me and certainly not for Edoardo. You know how he is, a different girl for every night of the week."

Kate's eyes squinted as if to see her better. "Yes, that's why this is all so fishy." She gave a slow nod. "You told me how much you hated his inconsequentiality where women were concerned."

"Kate, it truly is only a smidgen of fun on my part," Glory said brushing a lock of hair out of her eyes. "Trust me."

"Yes. Last time I did that, they stole the cutlery. Come on, Glory, 'fess up."

Tears stung her eyes and she savagely wiped her mouth with a paper napkin. "For heaven's sake, Kate," she said quickly. "Stop searching for hidden reasons. Can't you just once accept what I say?"

"Why are you getting so angry?"

She groped for her handkerchief. "Please, Kate," she begged.

Kate studied her shrewdly. Glory always hated it when she did that. As if she could get right inside her head and knew what she was thinking minutes before she thought anything at all.

Glory moved restlessly in her chair.

Kate's eyes widened. She drew back in her chair and stared open-mouthed as the truth hit her. "You're in love with him." She tapped her forehead with the heel of her hand. "I should've guessed. I'm right, aren't I? Tell me the truth, Glory."

For pity sake, how did Kate do it? Was she a mind reader? It was creepy. "That's not true, I don't love him," she denied hotly.

"If you don't want people to know you love him, stop wearing your heart on your sleeve." Kate studied the plate of sandwiches. "Do you want the curried egg?"

She shook her head. "You're wrong this time. I'm not in love with Edoardo," she denied. "And you can go on about it all day, but the end result will be the same. I don't love Edoardo."

"You'd be the most stubbornness, pertinacious, headstrong, and—"

"Kate, you flatter me," she teased.

She smiled at the waitress as she placed their coffee in front of them. Grateful for the respite Glory took a sip of the steaming liquid.

Then, because Kate was her friend and she couldn't pretend with her for too long, she said softly, "Yes, I love him. I love him very much."

And the words once said out loud became a magic elixir and stirred around her heart, nudged her psyche and settled inside her soul.

She looked around the cafe almost as if she expected everyone to stand up and applaud her open confession. Never before had she uttered those words aloud, *I love him.* They had always remained inside her heart.

"I knew it," Kate cried. "Oh, Glory, things have a habit of going haywire when one-sided love rears its beautiful head."

A one-sided love? Oh yes, she had always accepted that. She also knew she could never change the situation. Still, she made a last desperate stand. "Do you really believe I should have waited for my Prince Charming? I mean, you're supposed to be utilitarian. You're the one who's always crowing that you have a realistic hold on life."

"I think you should've waited for a bloke who loves you," Kate said sternly.

"Let it go, please, Kate."

Coldness settled in the pit of her stomach. She'd never known Kate to be so serious. Oh, she'd given her pep talks before, hundreds of them, but never with the same intensity as she was displaying at this moment.

Glory realized how much Kate was worried about her, and it endeared her heart even more to her friend. To get away from the subject of love and Edoardo, she said the first thing that came to mind. "I don't know what to wear to meet his parents."

Kate gave Glory a tilted stare. "Wear the black dress you bought yesterday. Can you remember that far back, Glory?" Kate chuckled. "I helped you pick it out."

"I was thinking it was too abstemious."

"Wear the black dress, Glory and tomorrow I want to hear all the gossip. Okay?"

She stared out of the window at the cherry tree. A late blossom fell from off the tree touching the ground like the first kiss of snow. "Kate?"

"Yes?"

"Thanks for being my friend."

She smiled. "I'll always be around if you need someone to talk to, you know that."

"Let's not talk about me."

Kate chuckled. "You want us to talk about my favourite subject?"

Glory grinned. "Yes," she said lovingly. "Let's talk about you."

With Kate in that small cafe, with the cherry blossoms trembling on the warm breeze, and the afternoon sun shimmering down on to the pavement, filling the cobblestones with rainbow mirrors, Glory spent two lovely hours.

They were, as they had always been and always would be, the best of friends.

*

Later that night, the idea of meeting Edoardo's parents wasn't easing her state of turbulence. She'd tried every avenue she could think of to get out of the meeting but to no avail. Edoardo was adamant. His parents wanted to meet his girlfriend.

Okay, she'd admit to herself that she was concerned this meeting the parents wouldn't go at all well. That somewhere, somehow, some way, something was going to get mixed-up and she would be found wanting.

For the first time in such a long while, Glory wished her mother alive. She needed the comfort and reassurance of an older woman. Whatever made her think of something as dim-witted as that?

Looking in the mirror, she studied her face. It was pale and rather anxious looking. Like when she was a kid and someone dared her to a feat that only Houdini could accomplish. She could dare herself not to love him, and that was possible, she was not going to love him — ever!

A current affairs program on TV caught Glory's attention. Oh, my God, it was about her and Edoardo. She watched assiduously. The press had had a field day. They loved her, and the polls were looking good, they couldn't stop now. Anyhow it was much too late to back out. The lie that they had begun had developed an existence and alacrity of its own, and there was no stopping it.

Showered, Glory slipped into a multi-coloured kimono and padded barefoot down the hall to her bedroom.

As she wiggled into her bra and panties, she looked at the dress she'd brought only yesterday, a classic long-sleeve black dress. The top featured a boat neckline and long slim sleeves that fell to the wrists. The shoulders and waist were trimmed with coordinating black beads and the skirt fell above the knee.

Since dating Edoardo her wardrobe had exploded. Not that she minded. It was fun searching for the right dress for the right occasion, a pleasure she'd not allowed herself for far too long.

She worked her long hair into a twist and pinned it up with a large silver hairpin, and then, with a curling iron, coiled the locks that spilt out from the twist. She held up a hand-mirror to admire the back of her hair. She liked the style, it was much more, dare she say it, glamorous than she'd ever worn it.

She threaded silver shoulder duster dangle earrings through the lobes of her ears, and da dah ...

Okay, so she needed to look good, give an extra-extra boost to her fast dwindling courage. And it wasn't that she wanted to impress Edoardo, no, sir-ee Bob, she needed to demonstrate for herself that she could look as female as the next woman.

She twisted around to glance at her back. She wasn't sure if she'd succeeded or not. "Darn," she muttered and sighed deeply. "To quote Popeye, I yam what I yam."

She left her bedroom, entered the lounge and slumped into an armchair. She could name all the places she'd rather be going to than Edoardo's parents. Like prison, for instance, or flying in a light aircraft over the Pacific Ocean with an utterly insane, out of control stunt pilot, or climbing Mount Everest dressed in a bikini and tennis shoes.

Her stomach tightened at the alarming sound of the doorbell. Reluctantly, she pushed herself out of the chair and walked to the front door.

He was wearing gray slacks and a sweater of pale blue wool that made his complexion appear more tanned. He leaned casually against the doorjamb, one hand thrust deep inside his pocket, a look of mischievous amusement on his handsome features.

He winked at her. "Are you ready to face the firing squad?"

"Will I be blindfolded?"

Beneath the thick brows his eyes regarded her appraisingly. They moved from the top of her head to the toes of her black strappy high heel sandals and back up again. It took all her willpower not to squirm or snap, *like what you see?*

Obviously he did because he said, "You look great," and without hesitation, he leaned over, ran his fingers over the skin of her throat. His touch sizzled her skin. She was on fire. And her love for this man flooded her like a tidal wave. Okay, okay, she never said it'd be easy not loving him, but she was trying and if determination was the key, then she would succeed. And then, in the very next moment, two seconds after self-talking and mustering up determination, she moved towards him, not quite touching. He linked an arm around her and she stood on tiptoes and brushed her lips along the stubble growth of his chin.

He kissed her, powerfully and lingering. They broke free. Breathing heavily. He wrapped his hands around her waist and dragged her roughly almost violently against his body. His hand boxed the back of her head and his eyes held hers as a wolf mesmerizes a prey.

He said her name so softly; had she imagined the sound of his voice?

He didn't kiss her again, instead he released her and she staggered a few steps back inside her apartment. So her determination had been tested and failed miserably. Oh God, what a wretched mess. She fought to make her voice come out relatively normal.

"I'll grab my handbag and coat." She left him and entered her bedroom.

For a few needed moments, she leaned against the bedroom door, fighting to bring back her equilibrium, her mind trying to come to terms with the reason behind his kiss.

How come she'd kissed him back like she'd been starving for his touch? How come her knees reacted as if they had been deboned? How come she'd acted like a gibbering idiot five seconds after seeing him at her front door? Bloody hell, she'd almost attacked him. What had happened to all that self-talk, the pat on the back that she could handle the situation?

She could blame it on his heartthrob charisma, his strength that glowed from the inside out. How could any woman resist him? How could she resist him?

Suddenly, she wanted to be far away from Edoardo, so far away that he couldn't find her. She didn't want to meet his mother and pretend that she was his girl, both of them clucking around him like mother hens, Glory feigning interest over a knitting pattern for a scarf for him to wear to a football match, smiling indulgently while his mum gave her his favourite recipes.

She gave an anxious glance in the bedroom mirror. She took a panicky intake of breath. "Everything will be all right."

What was wrong with her? She'd never fallen to pieces so quickly before. Okay, she'd had pre-trial nerves, who didn't? And going to the dentist wasn't her favourite thing on her to-do list. But she was strong enough to handle Edoardo Pisani and come out a winner.

Her self-esteem considerably restored, she returned to Edoardo. He was sprawled out in her favourite armchair reading a magazine.

She stood in front of him. "I'm ready, if you are," she said.

He stood, tossing the magazine carelessly onto a small glass-topped coffee table.

And they walked, with her slightly in front of him, like prisoner and guard on the way to the gallows, from the apartment, down the elevator and on to the street with barely a word between them.

Although it was well into summer an unsettling almost eerie wind chilled her.

She looked down the street. Leaves, old dirty, torn newspapers and dust were blowing in never-ending circles. The day was gray and forbidding, and the street gave an impression of desertion, as if they were the only people left in the world.

She'd be so glad when all this was over and they could go back to their rightful roles. And what was that? Her wishing with all her might he'd change into her Prince Charming?

Edoardo dating a new girl every week?

Her, Kate, and Aiden going every Saturday night to the local movie house and later pizza and ice-cream?

Edoardo's hand at her waist, she fought back the ridiculous desire to shake him loose, and tell him that she didn't want him to touch her ever again.

He opened the door of a silver Mercedes and she sank inside its luxurious interior. "You have a different car every time we go out," she said. "How many do you own?"

"None. I hire different cars."

"Don't like to be bogged down by possessions?" she almost

shot the words at him.

He gave her a quelling look. "Something like that."

He leaned over her to click the seat belt she hadn't yet fastened. He was so close she could easily wind her arms around his neck and drag his lips to crush with hers. She had no desire to kiss Edoardo. She'd kissed him enough to last her a lifetime. He was always kissing her. Didn't he always have his big hands on some part of her body?

Well, enough was enough and all that kissing and touching would have to stop. There was absolutely no need for physical contact of any sort. She moved uneasily in her seat.

As Edoardo slid in beside her, he asked, "How do you feel now about meeting my parents? Are you nervous?"

"Depends. Are they like you?" she quipped.

"Me? I hope not." He laughed. "My father simply adores my mother, always has and always will, and my mother's not prone to silence. She believes strongly in expressing her every feeling."

"Hmm, maybe that's a good way to be," she said reflectively.

His eyes were dark and glittery. "What would the world be like if everyone said what they really thought?" he said. "Like, I know your sister, she's the one with acute acne or, hey, of course you look great, just drop a few more kilos," he said with a ghost of a smile. "If we spent our lives being completely honest it'd only mess up the system."

"Then the system is safe with us, isn't it?" she said crisply.

"Why do you twist everything I say?"

"I'm not twisting anything, I'm just stating what I think." She was swamped by the intensity of her emotions.

His big hands gripped the steering wheel, and he nodded slowly. "Oh, I'm the big bad wolf in all this, am I?"

She glared at him with burning, fault-finding eyes. "Thanks for absolutely nothing, Edoardo." She lightly slapped her forehead. "I can't, for the life of me, understand how I allowed you to ambush me into this situation with your mother."

"Ambush you?" His voice lifted an octave. He cleared his throat.

Her eyes narrowed. "Do you know what bugs me? I'll tell you what bugs me. It's your superior, know-it-all, I'm-the-best attitude." What was wrong with her? She was spoiling for a fight, or maybe she was mad at him for putting her in this impossible predicament.

She tried to swallow the painful lump stuck in her throat. It made her voice come out all wobbly. "Like you're bestowing something wildly wonderful on me that I should be grateful for, ad infinitum."

She knew she'd hurt him by the way his head jerked back, but she had considered he was being careless with her, unmindful of her feelings.

He took a deep breath and composed himself. A brief glance at her. "I'm going to be a nice bloke and pretend you didn't say that." He was silent for a moment, and then he said, "You're smart, beautiful, and you never cease to amaze me."

"Wh—! What?" To cover her confusion, she said, "I'm not one of your conquests, Edoardo. There's no reward at the end of the evening from me." Her words were not as tartly spoken as she'd hoped. His compliments were singing through her brain. She'd liked what he'd said, very much. Well, what woman wouldn't?

"Sorry, just keeping in practice." That little remark brought her back to earth with a thud. Why didn't he use a sledgehammer? It'd be gentler. "Do you fall into bed with the men who flatter you?"

Now he was being intentionally cruel, and she hated him for that. Hated the feeling of vulnerability she suffered whenever she was with him. Hated that he could thrill or destroy her at will. She decided to protect herself by answering in the same cool tone, and with the same hurtful intent. "Sometimes."

"Do they kiss you as I do?" He gave her a slight shake. "Do they, Glory? Do they?"

He bent his head to grind his lips down on hers. There was anger in his kiss, passion too, but the anger was stronger as was his need to control her, to make her submit to his demands — whatever they were.

She pushed him away."That's none of your damn business." She took a silent vow that she would die before she would give in to him. "How dare you question my morals when you have your own tainted morals to contend with. You imagine you can do or say anything to me and I'd accept it as part and parcel of our bargain. How wrong you are."

She may be wildly in love with him, but she wouldn't allow him to trespass over the boundaries that she had set for him.

"Glory, I—"

"And what of the many women you've loved?" she cried. "How many? Too many to remember, I suspect? Have they all craved for you like some illicit drug that they can't get enough of?" Her voice trembled. "You have what you want from me, Edoardo. Ask for nothing else."

A hint of pain flashed across his handsome face. "What head games are you playing with me?" he growled. "What I want is to get through this and come out sane at the end. When this day is over I'm going home and drink myself into oblivion."

He spun out of the line of traffic, passed two cars and swung back into line. The tyres squealed like a cat in pain as he took a corner far too fast. She gripped the safety belt and refrained from screaming. He must have sensed her panic for his driving moderated.

She dared to glance at him. Edoardo seemed calm although his eyes held a fierce glitter. This was utterly crazy. Fighting with him bought no satisfaction, only an almighty headache.

She was tired of the argument, and far too stressed to care. She needed to get things back on an even keel. Their argument was superficial and meaningless. She'd started it, now she was sure, to get under his skin because she was so darn nervous about meeting his parents.

She took a deep breath through her nostrils, exhaled, and said, "I *am* looking forward to meeting your parents, Edoardo. I'm sure they're wonderful people." She hesitated, and then relented, "Like their son."

He seemed relieved that the tension had eased. "Thanks. That wasn't too difficult, was it?" He grinned. "Even if you don't mean it. They're excited about meeting you. You're the first since Sophia."

"That's nice," she murmured.

She stared vacantly out of the car window as the enormity of what she was doing overcame her. And, like him, all she wanted was for this day to be over.

Tears burned. No use crying, her mascara would run and she'd look awful.

They stopped at a red light. "Are you okay?" he asked her quietly.

"Yes," she said throatily.

"My parents won't bite you." His tone had a touch of warmth and concern.

Her stomach churned with anxiety and frustration. "I'm not worried," she lied.

"It's not like you to be so quiet," he continued steadily.

"Don't worry. I'm okay." She pressed her lips together and folded her arms.

He stared at her, then at the toot of a horn, flung the car into gear and took off.

They remained silent for the rest of the trip, each with their thoughts.

The abundant grape vines came into view, thick with luscious green fruit. She knew Edoardo's father worked a very successful wine-making business. His parents, according to Edoardo, had grown quite wealthy over the years and now enjoyed the fruits of their labour. She smiled at her analogy, wanting to share it with him, but remained silent. Maybe she was a trifle too nervous to share the pun.

Edoardo drove down a long winding elm-lined gravelled driveway and pulled up outside a large lovely weatherboard white-and-blue shuttered house steeped in the nineteenth century.

She moved with Edoardo onto the path. The sun shone now, the sky a vivid blue, and, except a cicada burred somewhere in the bush, the silence was serenity itself. It lifted her spirits.

They moved through the beautifully carved front door with side panels of colourful leadlight patterned in the shape of cockatoos and gum trees.

Glory drew in a deep breath and he glanced down at her. "Everything will be all right," he assured her. Then he called out, "Mamma, Papa, we're here."

He took her across the sitting-room until she was standing in front of an attractive middle-aged woman with salt and pepper hair and eyes the same deep blue as her son's.

Edoardo's mother was dressed all in blue. A long-line Jacquard cotton ramie weave jacket and chiffon cropped pants. On the lapel of the jacket sat, in all its magnificence, a transparent green enamel, diamond and pearl studded lizard brooch.

Mrs Pisani held out her arms and, as if it were the most natural thing in the world, Glory rushed into them. "Glory at last. Oh, *cara bambina,* the words will not come. You cannot possibly imagine how much I have been longing for this moment."

Her English held a strong Italian accent. "Here, let me look at you." She held Glory at arms' length. "Oh, Edoardo," she breathed, "She is beautiful, *si.*"

He gave a soft laugh. His voice low. "*Si,* she is beautiful, Mamma."

A tall handsome man entered the room. An older replica of Edoardo. He smiled and Glory automatically smiled back. He approached her, his arms held out, and Glory moved into them. "My dear, child," he whispered, "I cannot tell you how pleased I am to see you." He held her away from him, studying her face.

"Ah, you are so beautiful. Eh, Mamma, she is beautiful, *si*."

Edoardo moved in close to her, placing his arm around her shoulders. "Papa, Mamma, this is my girl." Glory gave him a swift glance at those last words. "Glory, my parents Silvio and Pina."

Pina placed her arm around Glory's waist and led her to a long, tapestry-covered couch. "Come sit next to me. We have so much to discuss, and so much to talk about. You work with Edoardo, don't you? His partner, *si*?"

Glory gave a soft not so nervous now, laugh. "Not quite his partner, Mrs. Pisani, more like his small fry. You know, the one who does all the work." She flashed Edoardo a sideward glance.

"Don't listen to her, Mamma, she runs the practice." His laugh was wicked. "Or so she thinks."

Pina said softly, "Edoardo tells me that you are an orphan."

Glory nodded crazily, like a toy plastic dog on the back seat of a car, oddly wanting to please his mother, make her like her for herself alone. And pleased with her son's choice of ... of what? A permanent girlfriend? A wife? Or just a show-piece to tag around on his arm, smiling sweetly at anyone who poked a nose in her direction? *Darn, don't go down that dismal path.*

Mamma smiled adoringly first at Edoardo, then at Glory. "Then you must look on me as mamma, and I will be your mother, *si*?"

"Yes, Mrs. Pisani," Glory whispered, completely overwhelmed.

Pina took Glory's hands between hers. "No, *cara*, not Mrs. Pisani. Mamma. Just mamma. You will call me mamma, *si*?" she insisted.

Glory felt terrible that Mamma believed her to be a real part of Edoardo's life, a woman who would be part of their family, but at the same time the warmth delighted Glory. The affection she felt from Pina was new and so sweet. It had been so long since Glory had experienced real fondness from an older woman that she had this rather childish desire to climb on mamma's knee, bury her face into her more than ample bosom and bawl her eyes out. Tell her how much she loved Edoardo and how he could never be her Prince Charming.

Mamma lifted her plump shoulders, straightened her back, and said, "We are so excited that you are marrying our Edoardo."

"Marrying Edoardo!" Glory yelped, her body jumping back an inch or two. She gazed swiftly around the room. Where was the exit?

"You are the first girl he has brought home since his first marriage ended, so we knew it must be because you will be married! And of course he would pick a wonderful lovely woman who shares his interests. We are so happy, *si*, Papa?

"Have you chosen your dress?" Joy bubbled in Mamma's laugh and shone in her eyes. "I know this wonderful seamstress who made clothes for Sophia Loren. Oh, she is old now but still her fingers are so nimble."

"What dress?" Glory asked. Things were going fast from bad to downright disastrous. "I don't know anything about any dress."

Mamma clucked like a mother duck. "Your wedding dress, *cara*."

Confusion weakened her voice. "I didn't imagine being married."

Her head was whirling like a crazy spinning top. She had no idea what was going on, had even less idea how to handle the situation, and could do nothing else than go along with whatever happened and pray to God that she would come out the other end sane.

This meeting was supposed to be the meeting of the girlfriend, maybe the possible intended down the track a few years, to Edoardo's parents. Glory had come totally unprepared to discuss marriage.

She flew an anxious glance over to Edoardo. He appeared as stunned as she. So why wasn't he saying something, denying that they were to be married? Explain to his mother that the wedding would come at a much later date — a much, much later date.

Mamma's hand flew to her mouth. "Not be married as a bride," she cried. "You wish to kill your mother?" She thrust her ample breasts forward, hitting her chest with the palm of one hand. "End my misery now and do it with a knife. It will be kinder."

"Mamma," Glory stuttered, "I didn't meant to hurt you. It's

only that we haven't thought about the wedding." She flashed Edoardo a pleading look, which he chose to ignore. What was with him? For God's sake, why didn't he come to her rescue? "I mean, we've only just fallen in love."

"*Si, si, cara.*" Mamma pursed her lips. "Now, the wedding. We are going to have all the trimmings, I am determined," she said. "And of course it must be a church wedding."

Glory lurched, ice spreading through her stomach. *Death, where is thy sting?*

"Please, Mamma, no church and no wedding dress," she begged. "I'll do whatever else you want, I promise. You can invite the Prime Minister, the Queen of England or the President of Italy, but please no church and no wedding dress."

Glory gave a tiny hiccup. She couldn't remember ever having lost control the way she had at this very moment, this giddy sensation of being swept into a whirlpool and spiralling downward fast. No matter what, it seemed she couldn't keep the situation in check.

On one hand she didn't want to hurt Mamma, and on the other, she wanted her to know that Edoardo wasn't intending marriage. Nor, by God, was she.

Mamma embraced her. "Hush, *cara*, we will not discuss the wedding today, if this upsets you." Mamma stood. "I'll be only a moment. Papa, please come with me."

Edoardo squatted down next to Glory.

Her eyes lowered. She could see the way the denim of his jeans dragged firmly over the muscles of his thighs. He was barely inches from her, and she had an almost overwhelming craving to reach over and run her fingertips across his mouth.

She swallowed hastily, moistening her dry lips. Her heart hammered. "Edoardo," she murmured, "Can you tell me in words of four syllables or less, what's going on? Your mother is talking about a bridal dress, a wedding and an organ playing *Here Comes the Bride*. What happened to the courtship and the long long long engagement?"

She breathed deeply through her nostrils. "I don't know what to say to her." He remained silent. "Edoardo, are you listening to me?"

Edoardo glanced over his shoulder, his brow creased into a quick frown, then turned back to her and said affectionately, "I think we should kiss."

She was too startled by his suggestion to offer any resistance. "Wh—?"

His arms locked around her as he fell onto the couch beside her. "For Mamma's sake," he said. "You know, show her how much we're in love."

She brought her fingers to her mouth. "Is all this really necessary?"

"Nothing serious." He took her hand rubbing his thumb across her knuckles. She shivered. "A friendly kiss. A colleague's kiss. A kiss of a friend to a friend. You know what I mean."

"Do I?"

"For Mamma's benefit."

"For Mamma's benefit?"

"Uh huh." He flashed a cheeky grin. "When she comes back into the room we should be touching."

He lightly touched her face tracing his fingers down the side of her cheek. "The touching's good," she murmured. "Keep the touching."

And then his lips brushed hers and a sensation so sweet, so tender, so utterly exciting overtook her.

Her mind told her to resist, but her body refused. Her skin prickled pleasurably.

She could hear the abrasive uneven rhythm of her breathing.

His large hand cupped her chin and held it gently. His tongue circled the inside of her mouth sending shivers of desire racing through her.

His mouth covered hers hungrily. She revelled in the strong hardness of his lips, and returned his kiss with equal passion.

They broke apart guiltily springing to their feet at the sound of Mamma's voice.

"Refreshment, *carissimi*." She entered the room carrying a tray of coffee and an assortment of tiny iced cakes. She looked at them. "Oh, you two lovebirds," she gushed. "Now I was talking to Papa about the guest list."

"Guest list," Glory repeated dully. Like it was a sworn statement she could make no sense of.

Where would it all end? What was to happen now that Mamma expected them to marry? She needed time to sort things out. Plan a definite course of action, a retreat with all bugles blowing.

"I think you're overwhelming Glory," Edoardo interrupted. "Let's have a drink and discuss the wedding plans tomorrow, *va bene*, Mamma?"

"*Si*. Papa, champagne to celebrate," Mamma chorused cheerfully. "I am so excited. You will come shopping with me tomorrow, *cara*, and we can discuss the wedding plans?" she said. "Oh, there are a thousand things to do before the wedding."

"Mamma, we didn't want too much fuss," Edoardo said hopefully.

Her fingers fiddled with the lizard brooch. "It will be simple, I promise you," she said evenly but determinedly, "but it will have class. After all, Edoardo, you will become Mayor of Melbourne."

"Well, that's debatable," he said with mirth. "I've got some strong opponents."

"You shall be mayor," his mother intoned, "and it shall be the society wedding of the year."

And with those words Glory's worst nightmares stood up and shook hands.

He winked. He actually winked at her over Mamma's head. What was with this bloke? He was the one screaming and yelling that he didn't want to get married, that marriage, home and kids was the last on his life's agenda. That he preferred the bachelor life and his little black book of who's who in his vast female kingdom.

He seemed, well, content, pleased with himself, smug even. What was going on behind those sea-blue eyes? What devilish plan was Edoardo plotting and, worse still, how did it include her?

For the first time in her life, Glory suffered the ghastly sensation of claustrophobia. She glanced around warily. The walls were closing in on her, and the room seemed as though it was as small as a broom closet cluttered with cleaning implements.

As her eyes searched for a fire escape, she caught the amused look on Edoardo's face, and the first true feeling of dislike for him entered her body.

She had to get out of this room or she may do something she would regret for the rest of her life, like knock Edoardo senseless.

Edoardo handed them their glasses. "To the four of us," he said raising his glass.

"The four of us," Mamma and Papa toasted.

Their eyes rested on Glory, as if they expected her to say something wildly wonderful. She raised her glass, gave a diminutive lop-sided smile that gave her, she was positive, the appearance of being slightly demented, and said, "Here, here."

And with a frantic wave of the glass, drank the champagne in one, long draught.

CHAPTER SIX

They didn't say much on the long drive home. Both, Glory imagined, busy with their thoughts and how they could handle Mamma Pisani, the wedding planner.

Even though she'd often imagined what it would be like married to Edoardo, when his mother had gone into full blast about the wedding, Glory had been, well, stunned.

Her dream had been of Edoardo declaring his never-ending love for her, and beseeching her to marry him and make him a happy and content man.

Glory had accepted long ago that that would never happen.

Edoardo pulled up outside her apartment, switched off the engine and turned to her.

His face was clouded so she couldn't ascertain how he was feeling. She was sure he wasn't pleased the way things had gone with his mother.

"Are you angry?" he said at last. When she didn't answer, he reached out and took her hand, rubbing it like she was an historical heroine who was suddenly light-headed. "Glory, let's talk about it." Patting her hand now. "Are you upset?"

She wasn't angry, she was gobsmacked. "Angry, no way. Edoardo, I'm totally freaked out."

She shuffled uneasily in her seat, a prickly sensation in the hand he was patting. Awkwardly, she withdrew her hand from his. No touching, evermore for any reason whatsoever was now her not-to-be-changed mantra.

They would remain exactly what this started out to be, colleagues helping each other out of tight spots, and when it was over and Edoardo was Mayor of Melbourne — as she was positive he would be as he was perfect for the role — they would resume their working relationship and tra-la things would go on as before.

Wouldn't they?

"I understand completely where Mamma is coming from," she answered circumspectly. "She wants her son married and happy, especially after your disastrous marriage. And she wants grandchildren." She sighed. "All mothers want that for their sons. It's only natural."

"I've told her over and over that I'll never marry again. It's like talking to a glass of water. She knows how unhappy both Sophia and I were. Knows what I went through." His brows drew together in an agonised expression. "And yet, she seems hell-bent on putting me through all that torture again."

"She doesn't see it the way you do," Glory placated. "Because she's so happy with Papa she thinks everyone should be married. She'd rationalise that something weird was wrong with Sophia, not with you." She took a deep breath, letting it out slowly. "I sort of think the same way," she said with a forced laugh.

"What?" A devilish look came into his eyes. "That something's wrong with Sophia?"

"No, not that," she said, irritated by his mocking tone. "You know what I mean."

"You really want the marriage scene, don't you?" he said, his blue eyes challenging.

She wanted to tell him how much she wanted a family of her own. How much it would mean to her to have someone to love and protect. But she doubted that he would understand. He'd fob her off as a incurable romantic or worse a dreamer of impossible dreams.

"Only when I meet my own Prince Charming," she said. A fine chill threaded through her as she wished she could retract the self-indulgent words. Whatever would Edoardo think of her now?

"The Prince Charming complex?" He chuckled softly, not in a malicious way, almost as if he understood where she was coming from. "Astride his white horse, ready to sweep his princess up and take her far away to his castle in the sky." He reached out to touch her cheek. "You can be such a mixture at times. One moment you're as smart and realistic as the earth itself, and the next you're rambling on about love coming on a white steed."

She pulled away from his touch as exasperation pinched her. "I meant it as a metaphor," she explained and wondered why the hell she was. He'd never understand her. Never know where she was coming from. And that was okay as she couldn't work him out either. Good balance keeping the see-saw even all the way along.

He studied her, and then said, surprising her, "I know what you meant and I truly hope you'll find him. This Prince Charming of yours."

He gazed at her and there was something unsettlingly sensual in the look, as if he hungered for her. "You deserve the best and I say that sincerely."

She didn't know how to answer Edoardo, she was quite dumb-founded at his answer, his complete understanding of what she was about.

"Thanks for going along with Mamma. You made her feel good."

"You allowed things to go too far," she admonished gently. "Your mother thinks … expects us to marry." She managed a smile. "Tomorrow she'll buy me a wedding dress, order the flowers, and book the church."

Glory gave Edoardo a steady look. "She's so desperate for a daughter and grand-children, she'll most probably buy heaps of maternity clothes, a layette, and a baby rattle," she ended worriedly. "I don't want your mum hurt in any of this, Edoardo. I couldn't handle that."

"I've no intentions of getting married, Glory," he said firmly.

Glory blew out a breath. "Then tell Mamma just that before it gets out of hand." Her hand reached out to touch his shoulder. She drew it back, and tucked it firmly under her legs.

His eyes connected with hers and a bolt jarred her heart. She lowered her eyes. She'd discovered that she couldn't stare into his eyes for very long it made her dizzy.

"She means well," he said earnestly, "but she didn't understand. I'll gently put her right." He paused as if considering what to say next. "You're everything she hoped my girl would be."

"So nice of you to say so," she said and grinned cheekily at him. She straightened in her seat and drew her lower lip under her teeth. "And when this atypical situation is over, what then, Edoardo?" she asked. "Will everything go back to normal? Can we still work together? Pretend that this never happened?"

"Of course we can," he threw away. "We're professional enough not to allow personal issues interfere with work ethics."

He gave her a shrewd look. "The way things are going, you'll end up a partner in the practice. I don't want to lose you, Glory. You're too important to m— the practice," he amended quickly.

Had she heard those words before this shambles started, how excited she would have been, but now, she didn't know, she just didn't know.

He smiled that oh so very very sexy smile, his eyes dark and glittery.

"You think me that good," she finally said with an odd twinge of disappointment.

"I know you're that good and you've earned it by your hard work and dedication," he acknowledged, and he flashed a fleeting smile before continuing with, "You've brought so much new work into the practice."

He leaned towards her, and she was enfolded in the smell of vanilla essence and it made her think of sweet ice cream on a hot summer's day.

Glory fought back the yearning to drape herself around him and lose herself in the intensity of his kisses and the command of his body.

*

Edoardo was wondering what she would do if he kissed her. Kiss her? Why didn't he simply drink battery acid? It would be smarter.

He wanted things to return to normal. A nod of salutation, and a how-was-your-weekend greeting as they met each other in the elevator.

This was supposed to be simple, Glory pretending to be his girlfriend, him achieving his goal of becoming Mayor of Melbourne and then, with click of his fingers, they would go back to what had been between them, respect, admiration and loyalty.

And he was vividly conscious that was what Glory wanted too.

Thank God, it was nearly over. It was October now, the election was a couple of weeks before Christmas. The inaugural ball was the week after Christmas and then— supposing he won? And he had reason to believe he would. Then, after he was mayor, they could pretend to drift apart. They both could relax as the practice closed down from Christmas Eve until the second week in January. They both needed this time to recuperate, and set their heads right.

When Mamma had gone into her spiel about the wedding at first he was amused. But why hadn't he stopped her before she'd become full blown? Why had he allowed the situation to get so out of hand?

It didn't make sense.

Of course he'd every intention of setting his mother straight, and, as soon as the time was right, he'd do just that.

He looked out the car window. The night was black and the stars were bright, like the stars in Glory's eyes when she was excited or pleased with something.

He drew in a deep breath. "Seems to me," he said softly. "I'm getting the most out of this bargain; me and Kate that is; doesn't seem quite fair somehow."

He turned his head and looked right into her lovely eyes. He managed to keep his gaze steady and even. "I wonder if there's any way I can make things up to you."

Glory didn't answer for a moment, until she said quietly, "I'm okay."

Her eyes were bright, her mouth soft, and the moon shining through the car window bathed her in a celestial light. She looked lovely in glow of the soft moonlight and he fought the intense desire to kiss her senseless. It was difficult for him to understand what was going on. He'd never had problems with women before. If he wanted to kiss them, then he kissed them and if it went further, great! No hang-ups, no tension, and certainly no arguments. So why did he want Glory in his bed? With all the angst between them why didn't he play it straight, shake hands and thank her for her time?

And another thing. He hadn't dated another woman since all this began. Hell, was he losing his grip? Was he, he mentally shuddered, thinking about buying felt slippers and a pipe? He'd have to be more remote from Glory, back to being work-mates. the slap on the back and how ya goin' mates. Yes, that was the answer.

And he found himself saying, "You're beautiful, has anybody told you that?"

Hell, was he completely crazy? This wasn't what he wanted to say; to the opposite.

She didn't reply and then, quietly, said, "Are you coming on to me, Edoardo?"

He couldn't shut-up; there was a tiny fat baby with a bow and arrow on his shoulder feeding words into his mouth. "I've never known a woman like you. Your sense of fair play, your humour, the way you'd do anything for the people you love. That's something else, don't you know."

She lowered her eyes. "Heck, Edoardo, you make me sounds like a saint."

"Saint Glory. Has a certain ring to it." He took her hand, rubbing his thumb lightly over her knuckles. Her hand was soft and warm and the impulse to kiss her was hard to ignore.

If Glory understood a portion of what was going on between

them, he would give his right arm if she'd explain it to him.

He didn't have a clue about why he was so deeply passionate about her, or why adrenalin rushed every time he looked at her, and how he had to fight the urge to run his hands through her hair, touch her in an intimate and possessive way.

Her eyes grew dark and his heart clamped in his chest.

Lately, every time he was with her, he had to fight the impulse to kiss her luscious mouth. He liked kissing her. And at this particular moment, he didn't feel like fighting that impulse. Her perfume invaded his senses, filled him with longing.

Edoardo tilted her head back, and then lowered his mouth to hers.

"Edoardo," she whispered against his mouth. "Oh, Edoardo."

He caressed her exposed throat and kissed the soft skin beneath her ear. The sweetness of her skin sent his heart pounding in his chest. He moved in closer, so close that he could see the freckles scattered across the bridge of her nose.

He lightly grasped her shoulders and began stroking her back.

It was as if he had reached a destination that he'd pursued all his life, some strange exotic place he had only before dreamed about.

Her hands moved up to his hairline softly kneading his neck sending hot shivers down his spine.

When he lifted her hair away and brushed the back of her neck with his lips, he heard the breath catch in her throat. Her hand was on his chest.

He took her hand and moved it so he could kiss her palm and then her wrist.

Never in his life had he wanted a woman as much as he wanted Glory. Now, this moment. "I want you, *amore*," he whispered.

Outside the car, a gentle wind was breathing through the trees as the moon disappeared and black night took hold of the earth.

Both were oblivious to anything else but each other and the burning need each inflamed in the other.

He took her in his arms and their lips met in a shatteringly kiss of passion and the world spun around him in a confused whirl.

Her tongue, easy and warm against his.

His heartbeat was erratic as thrill after thrill raced through him.

He moved his head until his cheek touched lightly against hers, her fingers softly caressing the side of his face.

Her head tilted forward as his seeking lips found the cradle of her neck.

The aroma of sweet roses filled the car.

A loud toot of a horn drew them apart. "Hell, Glory," he said as he brushed cupid from his shoulder. He wasn't the least sure what he wanted to say. Most probably something about how he had lost control there for a moment.

The night, her perfume, the close proximity inside the car all stirred his senses.

"I suppose you were thinking about someone else that made you want to kiss me?" she said and he desperately wanted to deny it. He didn't want her hurt or upset through any of this and it seemed that was happening more each day.

Instead, he murmured, "It won't happen again." But he really wasn't that sure.

"So you keep telling me." Her hand was juggling with the car door-handle. "I'd appreciate that you don't jump on me again."

"Put it down to the heat of the moment." She made his blood boil. She made him so that he couldn't think straight. She made him ... "I suppose I should thank you for being so nice to Mamma."

Now the door was open. *Don't go, stay with me.*

He couldn't take a chance on love. Not again, not ever again.

Marriage meant jealous hysterics and heartache. Marriage meant unfounded accusations and tearful scenes. Marriage meant control instead of mutual respect. Marriage was so not for him.

Keep with women who were only interested in his money and

being seen at the right places. Show them a good time, lavish them with gifts and wish them a bon farewell and move on to the next.

"It was easy being nice to your mother. I didn't realize how much I'd like her," Glory quipped. "Tell me, were you adopted?"

Then Glory was out of the car, and swashbuckling that cute little backside towards the entrance of her apartment block.

He stuck his head out of the car window and with a disapproving look, yelled, "Thanks for nothing."

Shoving the car into gear, Edoardo drove away at top speed.

CHAPTER SEVEN

"Here we are," Edoardo said as he braked in front of a tall, impressive house in Toorak.

The last week of October into the first week of November had been hectic and tonight they had been invited to Raoul Abdulhamid's for cocktails and light entertainment. Raoul was Chairman of Committee for Melbourne and supported new and ground-breaking commerce development. He supported Edoardo in his bid to be Mayor and had arranged this evening to introduce Edoardo to some very important people. Tonight was very important to Edoardo and the campaign.

Edoardo knocked on the door. They were admitted by a maid and ushered into a large room illuminated by a center row of crystal chandeliers.

The furniture consisted of low divans and cedar wood tables. Several people were seated on divans, others clustered around in small intimate groups. A pianist tinkled out Gershwin, while black and white clad waiters glided about unobtrusively.

Their host was a giant, prematurely bald and dressed in a black dinner suit and white open-neck frilled-front shirt. A red cummerbund encircled his massive waist. He reminded Glory of a genie out of a magic lamp.

"Raoul, allow me to introduce Glory Sandrin, Glory, Raoul Abdulhamid, our most gracious host."

They shook hands. "I make you most welcome in my humble home."

"Thank you, Raoul. I feel most welcome," Glory said. "I notice that you have some wonderful antiquities."

"Ah, yes, my passion."

"Me too," said Glory. "I've always been interested in Egyptian art."

"Hey, oddly enough so have I," Edoardo said. They were finding more about each other, they smiled.

"Then allow me to show you something wonderful." He led them to the corner of the room where, resting on a marble pedestal sat a tablet showing Queen Nefertiti bestowing a kiss on her daughter Merytaten.

"My God," breathed Edoardo. "This is exquisite." He studied the sculpture.

"Demonstrating feelings is most rare in Egyptian art." Raoul ran his finger across the face of the Egyptian queen. "Her features have been deliberately obliterated. A sign of the devastation visited on images of her and her husband after his death.

"I have much more to show you, Edoardo and you too Glory. Perhaps another time you could come for lunch and I'll show you my collection. I guarantee it is most breathtaking."

"We'd be delighted to come, Raoul, and much honored."

Bowing slightly, Raoul led them to a seat, which was barely above floor level. "Please enjoy your evening, and Edoardo we will meet with many people whose greatest desire is to meet with you, while the ladies have their coffee and talk as only women can."

"Thanks, Raoul, I look forward to it with pleasure."

*

Edoardo looked down at her, then at the low divan on which they were presumably to sit.

"Who's going down first?"

"Me, I suppose."

He grinned and watched her flop on to one of the brightly colored cushions. Sinking gracefully to the floor brought a sense of smug satisfaction when, almost without warning, he slumped down beside her. The weight of his body bounced her off the satin cushion, sliding her along the highly polished floor as if her backside was greased with oil.

His big hand reached over, grabbed the waist of her dress and tugging her back along the floorboards scooped his hand beneath her buttocks and lifted her back on to the cushion. "Sorry. I forgot to allow for weight displacement."

"I enjoyed the trip."

A waiter appeared from nowhere offering drinks and small savories. Glory accepted a drink while Edoardo took both.

At one end of the room stood a strikingly tall young woman magnificently dressed in a red silk strapless fish tail evening gown, the bodice clustered with Swarovski crystals, her long auburn hair was thick and curly. She held a violin. She smiled brightly at her audience, gave a slight nod of her head and tucked the violin under her chin. The atmosphere was hushed and energized, and Glory felt a prickle along her spine.

The woman began playing a section from Tchaikovsky Sibelius. How soulfully she made the instrument sing at the opening. Glory turned to Edoardo with a questioning glance, but he seemed rapt in the music. The music was making Glory feel strangely incorporeal. As the last note wafted through the air, she drew in a long breath, and closed her eyes lightly for a moment. As the musician moved away, her audience awarded her with wild applause.

Edoardo stood and offered Glory his hand. "Now that was something else."

"It was wonderful."

"Let's mingle?" Taking her by the hand, Edoardo led her across the room to where Raoul was standing with a group of people. "Ah, Edoardo, Glory. Please allow me to introduce you to Lord Havenish. Lord Havenish, Edoardo Pisani and his partner, Glory Sandrin. Basil is here in Australia strictly for pleasure, is that not true, Lord Havenish?"

The tall thin man, with a most aristocratic nose, smiled and said, "Is there anything else?" He smiled at Glory, reached out a hand, and clasped Edoardo's. "I'm also greatly interested in local politics, and you're just the fellow I want to talk to."

Around an hour or so later Edoardo returned to her and took her by the hand. "Boy, did he chew my ear," he said. "I couldn't get away from him. Nice bloke, though." He took her hand as if it was the most natural thing to do. People were taking their leave. "The party's over. Let's say our goodbyes."

*

Outside in the night air, Edoardo held the car door open for her. "Let's go somewhere," he suggested as he slid behind the steering wheel.

"Where?"

"Somewhere we can talk."

"Talk? What about?"

A smile hovered around his lips. "Work."

"We can discuss work at work," she said easily.

"Oh, come on, Glory. Let's go to Southbank and have a coffee."

Twenty minutes later they reached their destination. He helped her from the car. They found a café and sat at a table overlooking the Yarra River.

She glanced at his hands that were holding a menu. Strong, yet compassionate hands. Hands that could caress a woman with such gentleness it would leave her wanting — hands that would stroke and spell out a message of love and such passion that a woman would give herself to him totally, and willingly.

Her cheeks grew hot. She couldn't seem to control her racy thoughts while with Edoardo. She reached for a glass of water, her hands trembled.

"Any special type of coffee?"

She looked at him over the rim of the glass. "Short black, no sugar," she said.

"Something to eat?"

"Nothing, thanks."

Edoardo gave the order. Their coffee came and for a few moments they drank in a comfortable silence. "It's lovely here," he said.

"And popular on weekends. Of course, the Casino is a strong attraction."

"Want to go there?"

"Do you?"

"I'd rather talk."

"Me too."

"You've been great, Glory. I couldn't ask more of anyone."

"Seems our subterfuge is working, everyone believes I'm your girl."

He didn't answer, and then said, "Won't be for long now, only a few more weeks to the election."

His statement hurt her. She'd wanted him to say something wildly wonderful, like, *you'll always be my girl,* or *let's make this pretence real.* "Then back to normal."

"Whatever that may be."

"It'll be whatever we want it to be."

"Early morning meetings, penciling in court hearings, interviews with clients."

"You want something more, Edoardo?" *Say yes. Say, I do want more. Say, I want you, cara.*

"Nah, just rattling on. Another coffee?"

"No thanks." She moved her cup away from her.

"How about a walk alongside the river?" He held her hand as they walked from the cafe to the edge of the river.

They moved through a night that was suddenly mild and sprinkled with silver stars that reflected in tiny pools of light on the murky waters of the river. There was an easy silence between them, broken only by the tinkling of a piano somewhere in the background. The tune was familiar but its name eluded her.

She glanced at him. He was such an attractive man. His black hair tempting her to run her fingers through its wild array. His well-shaped lips could wander into such a wicked grin. And his magnificent liquid blue eyes — eyes that saw right through her. She had to be on full alert because she had this sneaking suspicion that his eyes could control her.

She turned to him, and heard the involuntary catch of her breath as his head lowered toward her — the wild beating of her heart.

He circled his fingers around the back of her throat while placing soft kisses all over her face. He traced one finger along her collarbone and across the soft material of her dress outlining the gulf forged by her breasts. Wild excitement pulsed through her.

Through eyes translucent with emotion, he met her gaze. Looking at him all but took her breath.

His kiss was a feather soft touch of his lips against her own. She felt the light touch of his tongue against her lips. Thrilling. Caressing. Breathtaking.

That he wanted to be with her as much as she wanted to be with him. That all other women past and future would be forgotten and he'd want only her in his life.

He kissed her brow, her cheek, her eyelid and back to her lips. Pleasure radiated through her veins.

Her body strained to receive his caresses. She felt reckless and very much alive and vital.

As her lips touched his, she felt them part. She could feel his tongue, light and warm touching hers, his quickening breath, as she pressed against his solid chest.

She felt as if she was being swept into a whirlpool of desire from which she had no chance of escape. Did she really want to escape from him?

She opened her eyes and a full moon shone down upon them, and she imagined its silver light spreading across the Yarra's murky waters.

The sound of laughter from somewhere behind them.

She could hear the gentle movement of the river. Smell the jasmine.

She thought she heard the song of a bird but could that have been possible this late at night?

And then she remembered the name of the tune — *The Best Is Yet to Come.*

And as his kiss deepened, she thought of nothing else but him.

CHAPTER EIGHT

Edoardo was coming to cook dinner. He'd tasted a few of Glory's shaky attempts at cooking, like her Chinese beef, where the beef always tasted rubbery no matter how much she paid for the steak, or how gently she cooked it; and what about her spaghetti marinara where the fish dissolved into a glutinous mess; or her charcoal sausages, onion and lumpy mashed potatoes.

Kate always said Glory's cooking was a burnt sacrifice to the gods.

Eventually, and most gently she had to admit, Edoardo suggested he take over the kitchen. What a delight. What a joy it was when Edoardo cooked. Suddenly vegetables had a wonderful flavour and a stew that used to have her shuddering at the thought, she now looked forward to with greedy anticipation.

Her mouth watered and she idly wondered what deliciously tantalising temptations he'd planned for tonight.

Glory had discovered that dinners were important to him almost a production number with the best china and crystal glasses for their wine.

She looked up at the bright blue sky and fluffy clouds. The day was surprisingly warm. Clad in a skimpy cropped T-shirt and short shorts, Glory was digging in her small and lovely garden.

Her stomach rumbled. She hadn't eaten a thing since breakfast, and she was ravenous. Tossing down the trowel, Glory straightened, placing her hands on her hips, stretched with a small groan of pleasure as her bones creaked into place.

She made her way into the kitchen. Opening the refrigerator door, she intently studied the contents eventually taking out a plate of cold roast chicken, bought from the local KFC on her way home last night for an easy dinner, a plastic container of left-over potato salad and a carton of milk.

She had no sooner placed the food onto the kitchen bench when Edoardo strode into the room.

"Hi," he said. "I knocked but you didn't hear me. Your front door was wide open, so I came in." He frowned. "You should make sure your door is secured. Never know who's lurking about."

"You were lurking about," she quipped.

"I'm not a mugger."

"That's debatable." He frowned. She laughed, delighted with his perplexity.

He was wearing light blue jeans and a stark white T-shirt that made his complexion seem darker, and had the appearance of a man who had just stepped out of the shower; his hair was damp and a thick black lock had fallen down his forehead. He looked so sexy that her heart pelted out a love-song in the middle of her throat.

He stood in front of her, big, powerful, and total male. She wondered how one man could have so much and not detonate. "You've got dirt on your nose," he said, wiping it off with the tip of his finger. He grinned. "I always seem to be wiping something or other off your face," Edoardo said good-humouredly.

"Been gardening."

"Nice." He stretched over, placing two plastic bags of goodies on the kitchen bench. "This is our dinner," Edoardo said.

Through the thin material of his T-shirt, the muscles in his chest rippled with every move he made. She swallowed harshly.

He squinted at the food she had taken from the refrigerator. "Eating and it's nearly five?" he said as he threw his long leg over a kitchen stool. He reached for a chicken leg.

She poured them each a glass of milk. "Get the urge to eat at any time day and night," she explained. "Comes from my ballet days."

He laughed. "You learned ballet?"

Fascinated as his strong even white teeth ripped the white meat from the bone.

She licked her lips nervously. Why was she so darn jumpy? Because he looked sexy, in a weaker position, as if she could take advantage of him and — and what? Attack him? Throw herself on to his body and beg him to kiss her, again and again?

"When I was a kid," she explained. "My mother imagined me on the stage. She thought I'd step into Anna Pavlova's ballet shoes."

"Show me."

She laughed softly. "Are you kidding?" She raked a hand back through her hair and exhaled. "My legs have seized up. Ballet classes were a long time ago." As if to prove her point, she stood and, placing a hand on one hip, shuffled around the room giving the occasional groan. "All my bones have stiffened."

"Indulge me."

She shook her head. "No way." She shrugged. "Anyhow I need incentive," she said, hoping to put him off his wacky request.

He rose from the stool, rummaged in the plastic bag and came back with a chocolate caramel koala in his hand. He carefully peeled off the silver paper. "Open your mouth," he ordered.

She obliged, he broke the chocolate into half and slid it into her mouth. "Yum," she murmured as the delicious taste of chocolate and caramel filled her mouth.

"Enough incentive?"

"You fool," she mumbled and made her way into the centre of the room. "Um, let's see. The basic petite allegro. Begin en face, right foot front, arms bras bas. Two bars four counts musical introduction."

She hummed an introduction. "Echappe sauté to second, taking arms to demi-seconde then two sautés in second, head remains en face, spring back into fifth, changing feet, bringing arms to—"

As Glory moved her feet, she lost balance and with a squeal tumbled to the ground. She immediately sprung to her feet, and cried, "Spring back into fifth, changing feet, bringing arms to fifth bras bas and collapse."

Out of breath, she sunk onto the stool beside him. "What do you think about that?" she gasped.

He clapped wildly. "You were great," he enthused. "I bow to your outstanding abilities. You're a woman of many talents."

"Too true, but—" Glory took a long drink of milk. "Don't ever ask me to do that again." She rubbed her lower back. "It'll take me a week and a half to get over it. I think I've broken my back."

He grinned and leaning over rubbed his fingers across her mouth. She jerked back her head. "You've got a milk moustache," he told her.

Disturbed by his touch, she rubbed the back of her hand across her mouth. "Please leave my grubby face alone," she said.

He left her, went to the radio and switched it on, fiddling with the dial until he found a station playing swing music.

Before she knew what she was doing he had her in his arms and they were dancing around the kitchen. Her breasts pressed firmly against his chest. Her desire for him flooded her like a wild river.

His hands slid under her T-shirt and clasped her waist. "Now this type of dancing I like," he murmured. "The I-can't-get-close-enough-to-you type of dance."

She should have drawn apart from him. Instead, she cuddled closer. He smelled wonderful, like summer rain on a hot pavement.

He stopped dancing and drew slightly back from her. He gazed down at her and her heart stopped beating, gave a hefty jerk and swung back into a mad beat.

There was so much emotion displayed on his face, yet she couldn't put a name to any of it. It confused and bewildered her and yet that he may love her flashed through her mind. Could it be true? Could Edoardo's feelings for her be deepening?

If he kissed her, whatever type of kiss — a peck, the kiss of a friend and colleague or a full-blown kiss of passion and desire — she would be his willing slave for all time. And you know what, she didn't care, for at this moment she was so full of love for him, her heart was bursting with happiness.

His head came lower and as his mouth moved closer and closer, her mouth opened slightly in readiness for his kiss.

The whole world stilled and everything disappeared and only Edoardo remained; gloriously alive, vividly technicoloured and potently sexy.

His face filled her view and his mouth pressed lightly against hers.

She melted into his arms like chocolate against her tongue.

The shrill sound of an alarm clock separated them like someone had thrown icy cold water over them. They quickly drew apart.

"What in—" Edoardo cried.

"It's my alarm clock."

"Set for five-thirty?"

She looked sheepish. "It's a reminder to have a shower and get ready, well, for you."

He chuckled, and then laughed loudly. "Sounds a great idea. I'll go and turn on the hot water tap. You bring the towels."

She laughed and knew he was half-joking. "And a rub down with baby oil, huh?"

He reached for her but Glory dodged his seeking hands. "You start dinner, Edoardo, I'm starving."

"Are you ever anything else?"

"A girl's gotta eat."

"Yeah, but there's a rule, only three meals a day," he said.

"I eat three meals a day except I divide them into two so I get six." She grinned. He laughed. "There's a bottle of red in the larder."

His blue eyes were alive with stardust. "Okay, run for the hills, but I'm a whiz at finding anything I'm dotty about," he told her with a ghost of a chuckle.

Wow, that was a nice thing for him to say. Heart thumping, she left the room to the relative safety of the bathroom.

Dressed in evening midnight blue wide-leg slacks and a white cropped lacy top, Glory had taken a few tresses of her hair, twisted and pinned at the back. Falling tendrils made for a casual yet attractive hair style.

He looked over at her as she entered the room and gave a low wolf whistle. "Now that's something else," he said with a grin.

Taking his compliment as her due, she gave a nod and said, "Just an old thing I threw on." She did a twirl for effect. "What's for dinner?"

Edoardo blew out a breath. "Compliments are so wasted on you."

"So feed me instead," she said brightly. "The way to a woman's heart is through her stomach."

He pulled out a chair. "Please sit and I'll bring out the first course."

As he was leaving she called out, "What is the first course?"

"Antipasto," he called. "What else would an Italian serve?"

"Yummo. Love it."

He returned and placed the platter near her. "Dig in," he said and she obliged eagerly.

"What's next?" she mumbled, her mouth half-full of antipasto.

He laughed indulgently. "Hey, enjoy the first before thinking of the second."

"It's your fault. You've got me hooked on good food." She patted her hips. "My hips and I thank you." She hesitated, and then said, "I think."

He laughed. "Your hips are perfect." She flashed him a knowing smile. "And the main course is Alla Carbonara. A special favourite of mine," he said, "followed by Fruttae dolce o formaggio."

"Which is?"

"Simply fruit and cheese."

"Hmmm, sounds much more interesting when said in Italian."

He grinned, and filled her glass with Amarone, a rich, dry red wine. "Wait till you taste my coffee. It's to die for."

"I've tasted your coffee, Edoardo, and my mouth shrivelled for a week."

"You're not suggesting it's too strong and bitter?" He held up his hands feigning suffering.

"Without offending your chef sensibilities? Oh my, yes."

Laughing they dug into their meals, not talking much until Edoardo suggested they take their wine out on to the balcony.

They sat on a large cane couch, relaxed in each other's company, talking about work, laughing over things that had gone wrong.

And there was something different about their relationship, something warmer, more exciting and maybe he was falling for her. That soon he would carry her in his white Mercedes to his castle in the Yarra Valley hills and make her his own special princess. She could dream, couldn't she?

Then he shattered the night by saying, "Will it be difficult for you, you know, acting normally back at work when this is all over?"

"What do you mean by that crack?"

"It wasn't a crack, it's a question."

"What type of question is that to ask me? Will I be normal? What they hey? Do you imagine in your tiny warped mind that I'll be sending you flowers and throwing confetti over your office desk? What's with you, Edoardo? You're the one who'll have trouble acting normal." Her breathing increased. "Know why? Because you're nuts, that's why?"

"I'm nuts? Wow, you sure have a way of twisting things to suit your own little needs."

"And while I'm at it, have you told Mamma about our so *not* having a wedding? Huh, huh? Have you? Well, have you, smarty pants?"

"Not yet, but I intend to and maybe tonight. Yeah, right, tonight."

"Good, and while you're at it, tell her and Papa that we're barely friends, and that working *normally* with you will be a hardship for me. Tell them just that." She leaped to her feet, towering over him, resisting the urge to pull his hair, or kick his shin.

He followed suit, and she bent backwards to look up at him. "I'm getting outta here."

She stomped into the lounge, grabbed his coat and threw it at him. "Goodnight, and I hope the bed bugs bite a hunk out of your backside."

He didn't answer, the slamming of the door was answer enough.

CHAPTER NINE

Edoardo eyeballed the pile of work on his desk.

He couldn't concentrate, not of late. Everything seemed out of perspective and he wasn't at all sure how to put things back in balance.

The way he was lately, it was a relief when he could hold a sensible conversation; it proved he was still rational.

He knew one thing, he was growing accustomed to her laughing face, and the peace she gave him and the way her presence made him feel totally alive. It gave him an odd, slightly daunting feeling of his life without her.

Until Glory, he had been in complete control of his emotions. But now?

Sometimes he would observe her lovely face in repose. Sensing his gaze, she'd look over at him, and he would quickly avert his gaze in case he would drown in the liquid fire of her eyes.

What the hell was happening to him? Why couldn't he stop thinking about her?

Edoardo picked up a legal document and began to read, but the words blurred beneath his vision.

Her kiss left him wanting more. And he remembered the way her mouth had tasted … soft, tender and sweet as honey on his tongue. Her softness and the undeniable scent of her. If he had to describe her in one turn of phrase, he'd call her earth woman. A woman full of love, generosity and kind-heartedness. A woman destined for children, home and hearth.

A woman he'd stayed clear of …

His eyes were drawn down the office desk-line towards her office. He could see her quite clearly, head bent over her desk, the silky veil of her hair covering her face, but he knew her face; could describe every freckle, every fine line of her skin.

Oh, yes, he knew that face so well.

Agitated, Edoardo left his desk and poured himself a strong black coffee, sinking back into his chair, he forced himself to work.

*

Edoardo, Edoardo, Edoardo.

Laughing. Talking. Working. Everything he was and everything he did haunted her like a lovely tune.

She imagined him confessing that he'd fallen in love with her and wanted her for his wife. She imagined them living in a white-and-blue shuttered weatherboard in the country near his parents and their children playing in a large tree-filled backyard, a dog barking.

She glanced down the office. He was working feverishly as usual as if there were only five hours in the day, his pen scribbling over sheets of paper. His legal mind alert and ready for any discrepancy, any loophole he could use to win his case.

Even from this distance she could see the darkness of his hair and the thick lock that dangled over his forehead. The width and strength of his shoulders stretching beneath the dark grey suit he wore, and she knew and loved the sea blueness of his eyes.

As he stood and stretched, Glory gasped, and drew back in her chair. He was looking at her, as if he knew she was watching him.

Frantically, she began writing on a notepad, and gave a soft chuckle when she realised she was writing a shopping list. Pushing the pad aside, she began summarising a deposition of the man pressing charges against her client. There was something fishy about his statement and she intended discovering what it was.

After a few minutes, she tossed her pen on to her desk, and pushed back in her chair. Tilting back her head, she closed her eyes. She couldn't concentrate, not right at this moment, her mind too full of Edoardo.

The startling ring of the telephone brought her tumbling back to the present. "Glory Sandrin," she said into the receiver. It was Jennifer at front reception telling that her client Margaret-Louise Lindsay was here for her three o'clock appointment.

She smiled as the older woman entered her office. "Hi, Mrs Lindsay, how are you today?"

The woman nestled into a chair. "I'm all right, thanks, Ms Sandrin." Then, the words tumbling from her mouth, she said, "Oh, Ms Sandrin, my son is innocent, and no one believes him."

"I do, Mrs Lindsay. I believe he's innocent," she said with strong conviction, "and I'll fight to the finish to prove it."

"It's been a nightmare, Ms Sandrin. The humiliation on the family. My son's employer accusing him of stealing money from the office safe. My son hasn't stolen as much as an apple from a neighbour's tree." She hastily wiped her hand over her eyes brushing back the hot tears spilling through her fingers and down her cheeks. Glory's heart ached for her client. "He's a good boy."

Glory smiled at that old chestnut *he's a good boy* spoken by every parent she'd ever interviewed.

Still, she did believe that Johnny Lindsay was a good boy, and that someone else within the firm had stolen the money, and she intended proving it.

The older woman handed over a cardboard file full of documents. "These are the items you requested. It took a bit of doing finding them." She gave a shaky smile. "I hope they're all in order."

"I'm sure they will be." Glory smiled receptively. "You didn't have to bring them in, Mrs Lindsay. You could have sent them by courier."

"I wanted to tell you something in person." Mrs Lindsay stood and held out her hand. Glory stood and the women shook hands.

"I know you'll help him," the woman said. "You've such a wonderful lawyer and a good person as well, and my family and I have great faith in you." She was stronger now, more confident as she added, "I know you'll help my son, Ms Sandrin."

"Thank you for your trust in me. I won't let you and Johnny down."

The woman left. At Mrs. Linday's confidence in her, Glory was stronger, more certain of herself and her situation with Edoardo.

She could handle being his *pretend* girlfriend as easily as she could argue her client's case in court.

And come out a winner.

CHAPTER TEN

It was Christmas Day.

And the temperature soared as the summer heat beat down on the city.

Edoardo's parents had wanted them to come to the country for Christmas dinner but he'd talked them around saying this year he wanted to do all the cooking.

Glory arrived at the Astor Apartments around eleven-thirty, looking up at the top floor where Edoardo's penthouse was.

She moved inside the large foyer and pressed the elevator up button. Inside she was entertained with television delivering news, weather and current affairs. "Must seriously consider upgrading my apartment," she murmured.

It was the first time she'd been inside his apartment. They usually went to hers as she'd told him she was more comfortable there. To tell the truth she was safer in her own environment.

He ushered her in by stepping back and sweeping his arm out in a half-circle. "Come into my parlour."

His apartment was, to put it mildly, spectacular. She admired the porcelain floor tiles and plush cream and beige diamond-patterned carpet.

He took her small suitcase as she'd considered she'd be a ball of perspiration by the time she'd got to his flat and would appreciate a shower and change of clothes.

"Want something to drink?"

Being here amongst his personal things had dried her throat as if she'd been without a drink for days. "Water will be fine."

He gave a wry smile as if he knew and understood her discomposure. "I won't be long," he said, "Make yourself at home."

She walked out on to a sunny balcony overlooking St Kilda, across Albert Park and Port Phillip Bay to the CBD. The street was so quiet and nearly deserted the stillness broken only by an occasional church bell and the rattle of a tram.

Back inside, he handed her a glass of icy water. The ice tinkled as she brought it to her lips. "Where's the bathroom?"

He jerked his thumb. "Down the hall, the second on the left."

She placed the glass on to a coffee table. Hmmm, Brazil-based Baita Design, a table design effect of tucking loops into one another, incredibly chic and playful but she knew however, more durable than appearance, it gave his lounge an elegant look.

She left him and found the right door. Inside the bathroom was a religious experience. She gave a small gasp. He surely knew how to live well. Floor-to-ceiling glass walls, bluestone vanity, glass mosaic tiles, all screaming taste and wealth.

She washed her hands, powdered her nose, added a touch of lipstick and returned to Edoardo.

He was playing Christmas music. Voices of a male choir singing carols drifted out. And in the distance she heard the soft cries of Santa's ho-ho-ho, and imagined the children's excitement as they woke up Christmas morning to gaily wrapped gifts.

She had always loved Christmas, the giving and receiving of gifts, the time when families got together and enjoyed each other.

Edoardo had dragged a large mahogany table into the centre of the room. He'd said he wanted to have the theme traditional for his parents in red and green with holly, ivy, and shiny apples.

He had made some Lime Vodka and it sat deliciously tempting, in a crystal punch bowl on the sideboard and beside it a bottle of Remy Martin X0 Special Champagne Cognac. He opened the cognac, and pouring some into a glass, tasted the glittering liquid. "Darn good," he muttered. "Want to try some?"

"Are you kidding?" she said, clearly surprised that he had asked her. "I'd be on my head and singing Dixie in less than a minute."

"Hey, Glory, relax a little, it's the festive season," he said jovially.

She smiled indulgently. "Oh, all right, but a thimbleful."

He handed her a glass. "To us."

Glass clinked glass. "To us." She downed the fiery liquid.

"How do you feel now?"

She grinned. "Warm and tingly."

"Another?"

She drew in a breath and blew it out slowly. "Wow, like later."

He glanced around the room, his eyes coming to rest on her face. They stared at each other as if they were seeing each other for the very first time. "What can I do to you — for you?" he amended quickly.

She smiled a warm and eager smile. "Stay in the kitchen and cook my Christmas dinner," she said. "The food smells really good."

"It is good." He wound his arms tightly around her waist. He walked her into the kitchen, stopped and looked down at her. "You smell good."

She stared, smiling, at his elongated frame, shoulders hunched in his white T-shirt and up at his handsome intelligent face. "So do you."

"This is great."

She was filled instantly with a sensation like warm honey rushing through her. "What?"

"You, me, here in the kitchen."

Her pulse suddenly leaped. She was glad she was here with him.

She remembered last Christmas and the Christmases before that she'd spent with Kate's family, truly welcomed and thoroughly enjoyable, but it still wasn't the same as having a family of her own.

She'd often wondered what it would be like to be completely surrounded by loving parents, devoted husband and children, so many kids that the walls bulged and the roof lifted from the noise of them.

She'd been alone for so long, but not this Christmas. Not today. Today she was with Edoardo and Mamma and Papa were coming and they would swap gifts and enjoy the meal and talk and laugh together.

If she never got another Christmas like this one, this would surely be enough for her.

Without thinking, Glory said to him, "Thanks for today."

His eyes widened and he cocked his head to one side. "What do you mean?"

"The last Christmas I spent with my family was the one before my mother died and it was never really festive." She ran a fingertip over the marble bench. "Mum was too sad to celebrate anything and kept herself locked inside her bedroom. I forgot what it's like."

She shrugged, wishing somehow that she had never started this conversation. "You know, being involved in the preparations. Waiting for someone special to arrive. Being with —" She broke off, not sure what she was going to say, but knew she was treading on dangerous grounds.

"Being with?" he insisted.

She laughed. "I'm becoming mushy. It must be the cognac."

He leaned over and curled a wisp of her hair around his forefinger. "You had it rough."

"No more than some."

His fingers moved down her neck and nuzzled along her collarbone. She shivered. He moved in closer and cupped her chin in his hand. His eyes were a startling blue. "I'd like to make things right for you."

She annoyed her bottom lip with her teeth. "You have," she whispered.

His lips brushed hers and her knees went weak. He whispered her name, but she barely heard him over the wild beating of her heart. His arms entwined her waist as he dragged her against him. "Let's not ever leave this kitchen," he said. "Let's make our life here away from everything else in the world. Let's pretend that there's no one else alive in the world, but us." His eyes were compelling, magnetic.

It was easy to get lost in the way he looked at her. "Your parents will be disappointed if they don't get their Christmas dinner," she said, knowing he would kiss her, wanting it, scared of it.

He turned up his smile a notch. "I suspect they'll get over it."

He crushed her to him in a kiss that exploded her heart and sent rushes of desire bolting through her like streak lightning.

She loved him so madly she would die from love's intensity.

A ting from the clock on the stove brought her to her senses. "If you don't attend to the turkey, we'll have to send out for pizza for Christmas dinner."

Edoardo exhaled a long sigh of contentment. "I adore pizza."

Joy bubbled in her laugh and shone in her eyes. "I'll go and set the table. Okay?"

He moved away from her. "Call me if you need me for — anything."

"I'll holler."

Laughing, she left him. He stayed in the kitchen for ages, wanting all the trimmings from bon-bons to a splendid plum pudding with brandy sauce. To provide, he'd told her, an impressive denouement to the meal and especially for his parents, Edoardo made panettone, an Italian yeast cake, tall and light and studded with sultanas with sifted vanilla-flavoured icing sugar to serve when they had their espresso coffee.

At one, she showered and changed into white linen shorts and pink silk shirt. For the hell of it, she boldly pinned a sprig of Christmas holly into the side of her hair.

"You come up well with a wash," he said as she strolled back to the dining-room.

She grinned. "Don't overdo the compliments. They might go to my head."

He pointed to the holly. "Is that there for any special reason?"

She touched the sprig in her hair. "None that I can think of."

"I can think of one or two. I can't stop staring at you." His laugh was soft and oh so warm. "Must be the cognac."

"Must be," she responded.

He looked magnificently male in his pale blue jeans and white open-neck silk shirt. She couldn't remember ever having seen a man so handsome. His hair was still damp from his shower and curled boyishly over his forehead.

Va-Va-Voom.

Dangerously original, shockingly potent and edgy.

A man with sharp corners and no toughness.

Athletic, smart, chiselled.

Whatever he had was enough.

Could he give up the other women and be satisfied with one — her? He seemed so loving, so close, so content to be with her that she was engulfed in dreams of Edoardo and her in happily ever after.

She reached over and brushed his hair back. "I like it when you do the girlfriend thingy," he whispered. "It makes me feel good."

"I don't know what you mean," she lied. She lifted her gaze to his.

"You touching me."

"I was touching you as a friend," she said, trying to ease the frantic beating of her heart. Looking at him all but took her breath away.

"I'm finding it harder and harder to think of you as just my buddy."

Gloriously alive, wonderfully happy knowing everything she'd dreamed of had come true. "It's the festive season it makes us all feel great. You know, Christmas bells, all that plum puddin'."

"You've got the cutest nose," he said leaning over and kissing the tip of her nose. "I want to kiss you."

"There's no law against it."

Stretching his arms out, he imprisoned her. At first he kissed her softly, his lips gliding moistly along hers. And then he planted his mouth over hers in a kiss of fierce demand.

Glory became torn by sensations. She returned Edoardo's kiss with force.

He moved slightly away from her looking down at her with a look she couldn't decipher.

She reached up to touch Edoardo's face, trace her fingers over the bridge of his nose and along his cheek. Her hand dropped and her palm came to rest at the base of his throat. She could feel the rapid pulse in his neck.

He quickly bent and caught her lower lip between his. His mouth demanded. They kissed hungrily. "It's more than the festive season," he whispered against her mouth. "It's you who makes me feel great."

The doorbell interrupted anything else he might have said. It was Mamma and Papa making their entrance, laden with gifts and bottles of champagne as if they were going to entertain several people instead of four.

"Merry Christmas, *miei cari*," they cried joyfully. "Is this not the most wonderful time of the year?"

"You look lovely, Mamma, and so handsome, Papa," Glory said, as indeed they did. The pale shimmer of an organdie blouse, the gleam of gold threads, complimented by a floor-length skirt of calico made Mamma look gorgeous, while Silvio was handsome in cream slacks, blue shirt, and a pale blue jacket.

"What about some of my special vodka punch, ladies and gent?" Edoardo suggested. "Get ourselves right into the festive mood."

Glory opened a gift of Cartier gold and diamond earrings that would dazzle the sun. "Oh, Mamma, Papa," she breathed, "They're exquisite and far too expensive. You shouldn't have."

"*Si*, we should," Mamma cut in. "Do not ever deprive us of the pleasure of indulging you, *cara*." She came and kissed Glory's flushed cheek.

"Can I get some of that loving, or is it reserved for women only?" Edoardo said.

The women laughed indulgently, both kissing Edoardo lightly on a cheek.

Mamma gave him a Dunhill silk tie handmade in Italy and Panama hat complete with a bright blue ribbon band around the crown. He placed the hat jauntily on one side of his head. "Well, how do I look, girls?"

Wonderful.

"It suits you, Edoardo," his mother gushed, "I knew it would."

As Edoardo gave Glory his gift of a papyrus, his fingers lingered on the palm of her hand. "Do you know the story?"

"Yes, I think I do. It's Queen Nefertary giving offerings to the Goddess Hathor in exchange for the Key of Life." She looked into Edoardo's eyes and when he didn't look away her heart took up a furious beat. "Nefertary was the wife of King Ramses," she murmured, totally spellbound by him.

"His favourite wife," he whispered.

"Oh, Edoardo, It's so beautiful."

He would kiss her; if he did and in front of his parents, she would kiss him back with every power she possessed.

And she was powerful. He made her so.

He made her realize just how wonderful it was to be a woman.

He completed her.

She never noticed Mamma coming to stand beside her, studying the papyrus, until she said, "It is authentic, is it not?"

"Almost," Edoardo answered. "Egyptologists, skilled in the art, reproduced the painting from archaeological discoveries of ancient Egypt. This is authentic papyrus that was handmade in the exact way used by ancient Egyptians around five thousand years ago."

"You learned that from Raoul."

"Of course. Wanted to impress."

"You succeeded. It's so thoughtful."

"I remembered you love Egyptian art."

"So do you."

He pointed to the painting and as Glory leaned over to study it more closely, he carelessly draped his arm around her shoulders. His touch was fire. "See how it shows the grains and texture each papyrus reed makes," Edoardo said.

"I love it, Edoardo." She gave him his gift of a silver fob watch. His name and the date were engraved inside the lid.

Mamma squealed in delight at her stuffed toys of a koala and kangaroo, which she immediately dubbed Stefano and Guiseppe and Silvio seemed pleased with his *Chanel Allure* range of grooming products.

Mamma began to sing Christmas carols. Her voice, pure alto, was pleasant to hear. Edoardo placed an arm around Mamma's shoulders and softly blended his voice with hers. "Edoardo," Mamma gently admonished, "you are singing the wrong words."

"Am I in key?"

"Practically."

He chuckled. "Then let's be grateful for small mercies."

Laughter filled the room.

Glory lay contentedly back in the large, soft couch next to papa and gazed at the two people singing, relishing in how much she loved them.

Edoardo, Mamma and Papa.

Such beautiful, wonderful words. Words like love and respect, commitment and honour, covenant and vows. Words she wanted to share with Edoardo.

She looked over at him and their eyes held for a brief moment before she lowered hers.

He was so dazzling, so physically powerful, and so resplendent, he took her very breath away. And yet, there was gentleness about him that she had recognized from the very beginning.

This time when she met his eyes she held them, a smile trembling on her lips and he returned her smile coming to sit beside her, draping his arm casually around her shoulders.

Leaning back against his solid chest, loving the feel of his fingers idly playing with the loose curls of her hair.

She closed her eyes.

She wanted this day to go on forever.

She wanted the magic of this day to live in her heart for always.

She wanted desperately to belong to these people for as long as she lived.

CHAPTER ELEVEN

Glory stood by Edoardo as they counted the votes. Her heart was in her mouth. She glanced at Edoardo. He looked relaxed, quite at ease, as if the whole affair didn't faze him. She admired his ability to remain calm, on the outside at least.

Then as the votes were counted and the announcement made, he reached across and took her hand.

Edoardo had won the race for Mayor of Melbourne hands-down. Her heart swelled with pride. There had been no contest as he'd won on popular demand. And now he had achieved his dream and tonight would be his night at his inaugural ball. A momentous occasion. An honour bestowed on an honourable man. And Glory wished with all her might that she could really be part of the new life he was bound for.

*

Edoardo arrived around six-thirty. "I thought you said eight," she said. "I'm not ready."

He shrugged. "I said the ball started at eight. I got here early to make sure you'd be ready in time." Plausible but somehow it didn't ring quite true.

He placed a bottle of Campbeltown whisky he'd brought with him on the table, and unscrewing the cap poured out a scotch and added a splash of soda.

"My feet are killing me," she moaned. "Your mother wanted to go shopping. I think we went to every department store in the CBD."

"Would you like a cup of tea?"

She glanced at him, surprised. "Thanks, but no thanks," she said. "I drank enough tea today to keep China in business for the next hundred years. But I'd like one of what you're having."

"No sooner said than done," he said pleasantly, reaching for another glass.

"You're not planning to poison me, are you?" she said light-heartedly.

He flashed a frown, "Can't I pour you a drink without you putting dire connotations. on it?"

"I meant it only as a joke."

"I didn't think it funny."

"I apologise."

"Hell, Glory." He threw ice into the glass and it tinkled merrily. Grabbing the scotch, he poured her a generous amount. He placed the glass under the soda siphon and pressed the lever with such force that soda splashed over the sleeve of his shirt. "Bugger," he muttered grabbing a napkin and dabbing at the offending spots.

Glory took the proffered glass, and sipped the fiery liquid. It was far too strong for her taste. She gave a shudder.

"What's wrong?"

She shrugged. "Nothing. It's perfect."

"No, it's not perfect."

"There's nothing wrong with this drink." She drank deeply. "It's delicious. Yum, yum," she said. "I've never tasted whisky like this. It's pure nectar. I can't wait to have another one."

A suggestion of annoyance hovered in his eyes. "You can be so damn irritating."

"Takes practice."

*

Edoardo didn't know why he'd reacted badly at her crack about the whisky. She simply got under his skin, annoyed the hell out of him.

He knew he'd never fully understand her, and if only he could fathom for one moment what went on behind those beautiful eyes, if only he knew the truth, then he could make his move.

A tiny sting of shock. *Hey, wait up.* What was he thinking about? *Make a move?*

Yet, he had to admit she fascinated him. She was so strong willed, so self-sufficient. He liked that in a woman, very much. And he liked the way her mouth moved when she laughed, and the wonderful fascinating fragrance of roses and lavender that lingered in her apartment.

Did this kissing-Glory-senseless urge go much deeper than he imagined?

He didn't want marriage. *For Pete's sake, remember what it was like with Sophia.* The constant harping about other women, the endless telephone calls checking up on him, the suspicion, the furtive searching of his trouser pockets for evidence of God knows what. He hadn't known half of what Sophia did or why she did it.

Edoardo only had to recall the heartache and utter despair, to make him marriage-proof. He looked over at Glory. And yet …

An expression of satisfaction showed in her eyes as if she knew something he didn't know. And that unsettled him more. Was he nervous about the inauguration? He doubted this to be so. Yet he had this odd feeling of something going wrong.

He knew that once the inaugural ceremony was over their deal was over, and they would go back to being just colleagues.

That's what he wanted, wasn't it?

Then back to the good old days when the hardest thing he had to do was choose which women he wanted to take out that night.

Glory seemed pleased with herself. "Are we picking your parents up?"

Her extraordinary rose brown gaze met his. "Papa rang just before I left work," he explained. "Mamma isn't feeling well."

Glory sat upright. "She was all right today. What happened to her and so quickly?"

"Upset tummy," he said. "May have been something she ate. She'll be okay."

A slight hesitation. "I'll get ready."

Her proud, erect back as she walked into the bedroom, completely at a loss how to handle her.

Standing, he walked to the window and gazed out at the night. He pressed his forehead against the cool glass and muttered, "*Madre di Dio*."

*

Glory entered the bathroom. She carried the constant craving to touch him, embrace him, molest him in a nice way. He exuded a disturbing mix of danger, melancholy and tomfoolery.

An intense excitement swirled through her. A certain knowledge that Edoardo loved her. Loved her enough for them to marry and bring their lives together in a warm explosion of love and contentment.

She whirled around the room, arms spread wide out, humming a joyful tune.

Slightly out of breath, she turned on the shower, stripped and stepped under the hot needles.

Towel-dried, she pampered herself with expensive body spray.

Wrapped in a silk bathrobe, she left the bathroom and entered her bedroom.

Here Glory dressed in a floor-length dress of the palest pink floral of silk chiffon with a soft deep V-neckline, and a much deeper pink, silk-lined velvet coat and deep red velvet shoes.

She wanted to look sexy and feminine and she knew she'd succeeded. She swept her hair into a style that knew no bounds. Complete with smudged, iridescent eyes and lip liner pencil in red under glossy lipstick in sheer tulip, she looked youthful and lovely.

She moved from the bedroom to where he sat in the lounge. "I'm ready."

His eyes deepened into wild violet as he said, casually. "Wow, you're really something else, do you know that?"

She was like a seventeen-year-old on a first date. She was grateful she had taken time to get ready. Since dating Edoardo she'd splurged on clothes. This dress was her most expensive and daring outfit. "It's nothing," she said. "An old thing."

He stood and moved in on her, taking her hands between his own. He stared deeply into her eyes. "Your eyes are lovely." He drew up one of her hands and placed a gentle kiss in the middle of the palm. "You're special to me," he murmured.

Heat soared through her body, and she resisted the urge to fall into his arms and kiss him senseless.

Her heart beat fast and hard.

Desperately needing air, she moved to the door and he followed her, not speaking until he parked the car in the Ambassador Hotel car park where the inaugural ball was taking place. They took the elevator to the top floor.

The clink of glasses and sounds of soft music came to her as they entered the foyer. Edoardo helped her off with her coat and handed it to the coat-check girl.

He steered her across a room that gave off a feeling of warmth and comfort. There was a cluster of about twenty or thirty tables in blackbean with matching blackbean and maple straight-back chairs with each table adorned with a floral arrangement of white orchids, tea-roses and baby breath, antique silver cutlery and matching candlesticks, crisp white serviettes and deep cut crystal glasses.

A three-piece band was playing mood music and an area had been cordoned off for dancing. It was all very classy.

He ushered her towards a group of people. "Paul," he said cheerfully, "I'd like you to meet Glory Sandrin. Glory, Paul Ostermann. Paul is the chairman of one of the biggest banks in Australia."

Paul caught her proffered hand in a tight grip shaking it up and down like a pepper pot. "Glad to meet you," he gushed. "I've heard wonderful things about you and it seems to me to be all true."

"Thanks. Edoardo has nothing but high praise for you," she said earnestly although she hadn't heard his name mentioned before this evening.

"Flattery will get you everywhere." Paul turned to a tiny woman with steel gray hair and bright brown eyes standing quietly by his side. "And this is my wife, Cynthia. Cynthia, Glory."

The women shook hands and engaged in idle chatter about life in general and Cynthia said how much she would like Glory to have coffee and cake with her one day when she was free.

The band started up dance music and the next thing she knew she was in Paul Ostermann's arms and tangoing around the dance floor like they had been dancing partners for many years.

Paul returned her to Edoardo. "You've picked yourself a lovely girl, Edoardo. You take care of her now," he said, slightly out of breath. "We're giving a small dinner party Saturday week. Want you and Glory to come. Around eight. Nothing special, completely informal."

"We'd love to," Glory gushed as Paul moved away to take his wife on to the dance floor.

He held Glory's chair while she sat, and took a seat opposite her. The lamps made his face appear more alive, pronounced the sensual curve of his mouth, and made his eyes glow a fascinating blue.

Hmmm, what a man.

Edoardo leaned over and laid his hand lightly on top of hers. "An invitation to his home? Have you made an impression. I've known him for years and never got past a beer at the club."

Glory was caught off-guard by the sudden effervescence of his voice. "So this invitation to his home is, umm, unusual?"

"Rare, Glory, rare. Paul's a very private person and his personal life is just that." Edoardo stood, came to her side, and held out his hand to her. "Dance with me."

She took his hand and he led her onto the dance floor. He slid his arm lightly around her waist. Light-headed, she resisted the impulse to lay her head on his shoulder.

He bent his head and she could feel the warmth of his breath on her neck. "Relax," he whispered. "You're all tensed up."

He may as well have suggested she pull out all her toenails, which would have been simple compared to relaxing while being in his arms. He fastened his grip, bringing her body into closer contact with his.

"Edoardo, please, I can't handle this at all—"

He boxed his fingers around the back of her neck pressing her cheek against the warmth of his chest. She liked it.

"Don't say anything. Not yet. Let's just have this moment."

Glory, unsettled again, sensing the vulnerability in this man. Lightly closing her eyes, she gave herself up to the music and the man; enveloped in his now familiar smell of cedar wood.

She was so close to him that every part of her body was touching his. She almost breathed a sigh of contentment. It was so good.

Raising her hands, she clasped them around his neck. He lowered his head and nuzzled at her neck. Unwittingly she murmured, "Oh, Edoardo."

His mouth moved to the lobe of her ear as his tongue flicked across it, her pulse quickened and the blood roared in her ears. She was gripped by an excitement that she could scarcely contain.

The way he gently held her as if she was made from air and he was afraid she would float away and disappear. Then he was crushing her to him as if he wanted to never let her go.

He loved her.

She would be his wife ...

His eyes upon her, she raised her face, his mouth coming closer and closer. No one existed, but Edoardo. No sound in the whole world, except their hearts thudding in harmony. Excitement, so intense, as their mouths touched in a kiss of sweet passion and tenderness.

Heedless of where they were, she returned his kiss with equal passion. She wanted to give herself to the man she loved beyond life, for all time.

She loved him, to Glory it was that simple. It would always be that simple.

All she wanted was to stay with him and make her life with him and, here at this moment, she truly believed that he wanted the same.

At the mild applause of Paul and his wife, they pulled apart. Still holding hands, they walked back to their table. Edoardo held a chair for Glory and took his place opposite her.

He filled her wine glass and then his. "You've completely bewitched my parents. They adore you. Thanks for that."

"Pleasure," she murmured.

He stared into her eyes. "You've made a big hit here at the ball."

"No problem. They're nice people."

"You're nice people." Edoardo emphasised the second word.

"Edoardo, I—" Her voice trailed off, as a tall, slim woman glided to a stop at their table.

A husky voice spoke, "Darh-ling, how simply wonderful to see you. I looked for you as soon as I came through the door and there you were doing a light fantastic on the floor. I was impressed, I can tell you."

Edoardo came to his feet a look of absolute pleasure crossing his handsome features. "Bunny, what a wonderful surprise."

Bunny? As in Bugs? The corner of Glory's mouth pulled downward. She studied the platinum blonde with a wonderful slender figure, tall and imperial. Her eyes were jewel-green. The wide-lapelled jacket was a knockout in turquoise, while her clinging mini dress was perfect for cocktails in black satin.

How did she put it on? With a spray gun?

With her magazine cover looks she makes it all look so easy, Glory decided ungraciously.

She squirmed in her chair. Bunny was a sexy woman who obviously lived on celery sticks and raw carrot strips, with the occasional sip of extra dry white wine. Glory took a silent vow to give up fish and chips from this day forward and definitely no more ice coffee with the extra dollop of ice-cream, no matter what.

"What are you doing here?" Edoardo said. "You're the last person I expected to see."

Bunny laughed softly giving an almost tinkling sound. "I'd read where you'd made Lord Mayor, and I was totally impressed. Max Hadwell and his wife, Glenys, asked me to join them. Naturally I eagerly accepted." A quick, bored to tears glance had Glory closing her eyes and tilting her head back to stare at the magnificent crystal chandelier.

She idly wondered how the cleaners could get so high to dust it. What a strange thought.

Bunny didn't take a seat but remained standing, folding her arms across her tiny pert breasts. "Are you glad I came, Edoardo?"

His Adam apple played see-saw with his tonsils. Glad to see Bunny, ecstatic, almost drooling at the mouth. Glory wanted to reach out and take hold of his arm, but she knew that in all probability it wasn't a good idea.

"I had no idea you were home. How long have you been back from UK?" he asked.

"Two weeks," she kept her tone even. "I've been as busy as all hell."

"Two weeks," he repeated.

Bunny gave a bleak sigh. "I telephoned to make arrangements to go with you to the ball, but you never returned my calls."

"Sorry about that." Edoardo tightened the knot of his pure silk tie. "Been busy too and haven't been in the office much."

She smiled indulgently. "I rang your mobile several times."

He hesitated measuring her for a moment. "Yes, right," he said.

Bunny pursed her mouth into a rather petulant childlike shape and without being completely aware Glory parodied Bunny's facial expression.

Edoardo and Bunny acted like old friends who, knowing each other intimately needed only the fewest of words to communicate, the slightest touch to know how the other was feeling, and the familiarity of woven pasts.

Glory's heart ached, helpless as Edoardo smiled compassionately at Bunny.

His low voice was a little awkward. "I feel I've let you down."

Bunny tinkled that incongruous laugh that irritated Glory. "Don't be absurd." She glanced over her shoulder as if someone had called her name.

Her razor-sharp green eyes came back to rest on Glory. Bunny's chin tilted haughtily, her eyes heavily made up, and her expression that of a beautiful woman used to receiving the accolade of her admirers.

She was elegant, poised and totally confident of her power as a woman. "I've landed this wonderful contract for my lingerie," Bunny was saying, "and if everything goes the way I plan —" The laugh suggesting that nothing would dare get in the way of anything Bunny planned, "I could be living in Paris by summer."

"Paris? You've just returned from England," he protested.

He took Bunny's small white hand, and caressed it between his own. They stared into each other's eyes, this handsome, made-for-each-other couple, a rush of covetousness stir inside Glory.

Fickle-hearted rat.

How could I ever imagine that he loved me?

Will the real Edoardo Pisani please stand up? Well, he was and he's holding hands with his latest conquest. Charming her. Admiring her. Wanting her?

Again Bunny laughed showing tiny snow-white teeth and firm pink gums, and gave him a familiar little push. "You could join me in Paris for a few days," she suggested. "We could see the sights. Have a few laughs. Have some quality time together."

Quality time? Oh yes, like a day or three in bed, and only coming up for air and water.

"It's been too long," Bunny was saying. "I've missed you." She threw a glance at Glory that shouted that Bunny had just found half a worm in her apple.

Glory tried to place a ho-hum who-cares and this-is-so-boring-I'm-fighting-sleep look on her face. She failed miserably.

She suffered a primitive sensation of wanting to scratch Bunny's eyes out. Kick her in her fabulous shins. Claw her hands through Bunny's perfectly coiffure hair. *Her hair's dyed,* she decided smugly, *and she's got on enough make-up to sink the Titanic.*

Her heart clamped in her chest. She had to admit that Bunny looked wonderfully glamorous.

"You look incredibly gorgeous," Edoardo said. "You never change."

Oh, great, and I look like the local bag lady?

A tiny volcano of anger erupted.

Right, Pisani, this means war.

As his head tilted down towards Bunny's face, his black hair complimenting Bunny's blonde hair, a green-eyed monster waltzed around Glory's head, tugging at her ear, scratching at her brain, tantalizing her by whispering in her ear; *he's going to kiss Bunny; he's forgotten you already.*

You see, you idiot, kissing you meant totally nothing to him. He handed out his kisses like they were chocolates in a box.

He was coming onto Bunny as if their weeks of parting had never existed. As if they were alone in this room, and as if he should have her in his arms.

Crime passional.

It's as if I'm not here. I could be swinging from the chandelier singing Italian love songs in Greek and I'd be lucky if he noticed me.

"I don't think you've missed me one bit, Edoardo," Bunny said.

Okay, enough is enough. I'm here, I'm real and I'm darn well hurting.

Glory's cough was strong enough to hurt her throat.

This time Edoardo glanced at her, with a tried and found wanting expression on his handsome face.

An immediate wringing throb and Glory tried to swallow the lump that lingered in her throat.

Glory sighed, gripped her hands together, and stared at them.

"Oh," he murmured like he'd just realised she was there. "Glory, this is Bunny Baxter, Bunny, Glory Sandrin, a colleague of mine from work." Had he stressed the word colleague? Wasn't she supposed to be his girlfriend? The lucky one with the ring nearly on the fourth finger of her left hand?

And Bunny Baxter? Who had a name like Bunny Baxter? Sounds like an Easter egg slogan. Hey, kids, get your Bunny Baxter Easter egg here.

Glory smiled as sweetly as her mouth would allow. "Edoardo has told me so much about you," she gushed generously.

"Has he? Hmm, I'm so thrilled, especially when he hasn't said a thing about you," came Bunny's quick and rather spiteful reply.

Glory heard his voice and bit her bottom lip. "There's so much to tell you, Bunny," Edoardo was explaining. Why was he explaining? "We need time to talk. So much has happened that needs explaining."

He tugged at the collar of his shirt and both women smiled benevolently at his obvious discomfort. "I don't want you to misunderstand this situation," he continued, "but here isn't the place to talk about it."

Playboy extraordinaire. Well, hadn't she always known it? What a fool. What a dreamer. No more, back to normality with a heavy dose of realism.

Will the level-headed and sensible Glory Sandrin, please stand up.

"You know my address," she heard Bunny say. "Call by anytime."

How dare they talk around her as if she didn't matter? She swallowed hard, trying not to reveal her fast-growing anger.

Glory knew what it was like to be a shrew now, a spitfire, as angry as a disturbed hornet's nest. Her brow knitted of its own accord and heat surged and burned her cheeks.

And when Edoardo placed an arm around Bunny's shoulders and lowering his voice said conspiratorially, "This isn't what you think," Glory was thirsting for revenge. She was implacable, irreconcilable, and unappeasable.

She wanted payback. She wanted atonement. She wanted to see herself as the victor and Edoardo and Bunny as the victims. She wanted revenge with a capital R, and she wanted it *now*.

The words tumbled out of her mouth like a collapsing house of cards. "Edoardo, my own precious darh-ling," she cooed. "Perhaps Bunny would like to join us for a drink?"

"Yes." His teeth parted in a dazzling display of straight, white teeth. "Good thinking."

Before Edoardo could say another word, or Bunny take the proffered seat, Glory sang, "It's a celebration, Bunny. Isn't it, my own sweet heart?"

She fluttered her eyelashes at Edoardo. "Tell Bunny all about us, puddin' plum."

"A celebration?" Bunny repeated uncertainly. "What are you celebrating, Edoardo?"

"Sugar wooga," Glory hurried on, "you haven't told Bunny your playing days are over." She mimicked Bunny's voice. "You, naughty, naughty boy."

Only a flash of amazement crossed Bunny's beautiful features but it was enough to give Glory a fleeting sensation of satisfaction and some of the anger, not much, but some scattered.

"Serious, Edoardo?" Bunny said. "You've taken my breath away."

Before Edoardo could say another word, Glory, feeling totally in control and power-imbued, simpered, "It was love at the very first sight, Bunny. And now we just can't keep our hands off each other. Isn't that the downright truth, precious?" How come she was sounding like Scarlett straight from Tara? "We simply make love all night and most of the day, don't we, hot stuff? Why he just blows the socks right off my feet."

Bunny gave Edoardo a rather wry smile. "I guess this means Paris is out?"

"Bunny," he said imploringly, "We have to talk. I need to explain."

"I can hardly wait." She spoke to Glory. "It was great meeting you."

Bunny walked away, he had an expression on his face that suggested he'd just discovered he had a terminal disease. He abruptly sat. "Bunny is a friend of mine."

"I bet," she scorned. "I'm not sure but I think I hate her."

"I happen to like her." He moved his shoulders.

Glory shrugged. "So?"

"I never imagined meeting her this way. Damn, whatever I tell her will sound lame." His fingers tapered and long, tapped a message out on a crystal glass. "She may not believe me."

"How devastating," Glory drawled. "Pass me the butter knife while I cut my wrists."

"What was all that gibberish?" He bent his head slightly forward. "You sounded like a demented teenager."

Her nerves frayed now as she said, "Just playing the devoted girlfriend, Edoardo, that's what I thought you wanted me to do."

"Not with as much gusto." He moved restively in his chair. "Anyway you were downright rude."

Her mouth gaped slightly. "Huh, huh! And you weren't? Drooling down memory lane. Why, you couldn't even introduce me as your girlfriend. I could have been on another planet for all you cared."

"Sometimes I can't work you out," he said.

She gave him a dismissive look. Him with come-and-get-it eyes. "Why?"

He looked, well, mischievous and the look made her wonder what he had up his sleeve. "You think everything I do is some evil scheme."

"And it's not?" Her voice was shakier than she would have liked.

And then he pulled back in his chair and grinned. She didn't like the way he smiled. It was a smirk actually, almost victorious. The infallible-cat-that-drank-the-cream smirk and it sure did irritate the hell out of her.

"The way you acted with Bunny," he said, "I'd say you were jealous."

She pointed to her chest. "Me? Me, jealous? Hardy-ha-ha-ha, what a joke." She made a harsh sound. "What are you going on about? Jealous of Bunny? Who are you kidding? Why, I don't have a jealous bone in my body." She stopped and gulped.

"I don't like being ignored," she continued in a rush. "Nobody likes being ignored. How would you like it if a boyfriend of mine came along side and he ignored you? Hey? Hey? What about that, hey?"

For pity sake, I'm losing it.

"Take it easy. Unruffle your feathers." Again that infuriating look on his face, that gave the impulse to throw her glass of wine into his smirking features. "Care for some more wine?"

Glory abruptly stood. "If you don't mind, I'd like to go home."

He grinned. "Well, you can't," he said with a soft chuckle. "I have to stay here until everyone else leaves. So sit down and behave yourself."

She sat. "Behave myself? You really are the limit. You throw your girlfriend in my face and then tell me to behave myself. Why I'd rather be sitting here with a dog with rabies than with—"

He rose in his chair, leaned over the table and kissed her full on the mouth. She tried to ignore the shivers of desire racing through her as his tongue traced the soft fullness of her lips.

He pulled back and grinned. "Now, shut up and enjoy yourself."

She did as he said because quite frankly she didn't know what to say or what to do.

*

Edoardo was stunned. Glory was jealous. There was no denying the heat of her emotions, and oddly he liked it; liked that she was jealous and angry over another woman. He wanted to tell her that Bunny was nothing compared to her, and that his flitting from woman to woman was pure cowardice. He knew Glory and knew she wasn't Sophia. Sophia was a spoilt child who stamped her foot, at the slightest refusal of her demands. Glory was a woman who'd place her family first and foremost. Glory was a woman he could spend the rest of his life with. He knew this now. Hell, maybe he'd known it forever.

CHAPTER TWELVE

Edoardo followed Glory into her apartment, but she turned to him and said, "You can go now. You've got what you wanted. Done deal."

They stared at each other across a sudden ringing silence, until he said, "Glory, please."

"I've kept my end of the bargain," she said. "What's the use of going on with it?" She hesitated, torn by conflicting emotions. "This is it, the end of the line."

He pushed back her hair and kissed her forehead, her upper cheeks, and lightly upon her mouth. Love surged through her like a tidal wave, as he kissed her over and over. "I loved the way you handled Bunny," he said. "I love your spirit, your zest."

Surprise at his words of praise sluiced through. She couldn't get her head around what Edoardo was saying. "Wh—What?"

His expression was a mixture of admiration and, dare she say it … think it … hope for it — love.

"Seeing you with her, there's no comparison. You make every other woman fade into insignificance." His large hand took hold of her face and held it gently. "The way you are. The way you think. The things you do and say are all magic to me."

"Edoardo," she hesitated, blinking with bafflement. "What are you saying to me?"

"Something important. Something that will change our lives forever," he said. "You make me think seriously about all the things I was afraid of. Like having a wife, a home and kids."

His lips were upon hers. Sweet, hard, demanding. His tongue slipped into her mouth and her response was vibrant. She curved into him, wanting more of his kiss, never having enough of his embrace.

He pulled back slightly and said, "I'm in love with you. I want to marry you."

His eyes were a blue flame of passion; a passion so potent that it would surely burn her into eternity.

Then, as his words came home and warmed her cold heart, a quick rush of excitement rushed through her. Her arms were still wound around his neck, her body still cemented to his as if she would never let him go.

He relaxed his hold on her, raised a hand to her face and softly ran his fingertip from her cheek to her chin. His eyes searched her face, and then he reached out and took her face in his big hands. "You're so lovely," he murmured, and there was a caring in his voice. "I loved you from the beginning. I just didn't know it, not then," he said. "I was too scared to see love.

"You've made me believe again," he said in a low soft voice. "You've made me know there's a chance for me for happiness."

A thrill of excitement ran over her skin like summer lightning.

"Everything is right since I met you," he said. One finger caressed the top of her shoulder. "From the very first day I met you."

His lips touched her like a whisper. "I want to be good for you. I want to watch over you. I want to pamper you."

He left her breathless. "Oh, Edoardo, I've always loved you."

"Have you?"

She nodded. "From the moment I stepped inside your office."

His amazing blue gaze met hers. "I want to say sorry." He sank onto the couch bringing her with him.

"Me too," she apologised. "I acted like a first-class shrew."

His smile was so gentle. "About what happened at the mayoral ball," he began. "Bunny means nothing to me; no other woman on earth means anything to me except you. You mean everything to me."

"The way you spoke to her, so familiar, so loving and I thought you were trying to explain me away," she said questioningly.

"I was trying to explain but not how you think," he said. "I wanted her to know how much you meant to me and that my playing days were over. It wasn't the right time or place."

Oh, his face so familiar, so reassuring and so utterly dear. "I love you," she said softly.

"I thought you didn't love me."

She grinned as happiness flowed through her. "I thought you didn't love me."

"What fools we were." His laugh was victorious. "All my life, I believed love made you weak, and my marriage to Sophia confirmed it for me, so I fought against love," he said. "And now I know the power of love, and I never want to lose it, ever."

Through the unshaded window moonlight flooded and spread dancing creamy light across the polished floor and she imagined the stars blinking down on them. "I've always loved you."

"Me too." He ran his fingers down her throat and along the creamy texture of her shoulder. "You've the kindest, sweetest, most original and independent person I know." He kissed her forehead. He kissed her eager mouth. "You're all the woman I'll ever need and want." He gathered her into his arms.

"Let's have lots of fat babies. Let's buy a house in the country. Let's get old together." He slipped from the couch and knelt on one knee in front of her. He took her hand, kissing her soft knuckles. "What do you say, my love? Will you marry me?"

She leaned forward and kissed his mouth and her heart thumped wildly. "I say yes, I will marry you." She gave a wry smile. "Mamma can have her big fancy wedding and invite as many people as she wants. I'll even wear a fluffy white bridal gown."

Edoardo rose from his kneeling position. "She'll love that."

He came so close she could see the fine lines at the corner of his eyes. The hypnotic blue of his eyes overpowered her. She leant forward and lightly kissed his mouth. "And I want Kate to give me away."

"Who else?"

"And Aiden to be my page boy." There was a trace of laughter in her voice.

He nodded, considering. "Please tell me Kate will dress middle-of-the-road."

"Don't think so." She poked her cheek with her tongue. "She's very fond of sparkling sequins."

"Lord have mercy," he said and grinned.

"Kate will want to entertain the guests," she said with a grin.

He pulled back from her. "How?"

"She does a mean impersonation of Judy Garland and outdoes Fred Astaire with her tap-dancing." She ran her fingers through his thick hair.

His blue eyes were humorous and tender. "I'm totally impressed."

"You should be," she said earnestly. "Talent runs in my family."

There was a slight tinge of wonder in his voice. "And they are your family."

"Yes, they are."

"And now we'll join and become one big happy family." His soft voice urged her.

Contentedly she rested against the warmth of his body. "Oh yes, that would be wonderful."

His scent clean and profoundly masculine. Little prickles of fire, as his fingers traced lazy patterns on her arm.

His touch was reassuring. "Oh, Edoardo, you were such a mystery to me."

"Even when I didn't like you, I loved you." His grin was infectious. "You called me God-awful names. Thought the worst of me."

"Maybe that was true yesterday," she said, "but it's not true today."

He kissed her eager mouth. With one quick movement Edoardo pulled her to him. His voice was husky, his breath warm and sweet on her cheek.

"You unlocked something in my heart." His deep voice simmered with barely checked passion. "Made me feel something I thought I'd never feel again."

He held her against him, holding her as if she were more precious than gold. His mouth covered hers hungrily, and his kiss sent new spirals of ecstasy through her.

She arched into the curve of his body as his tongue playfully traced the outline of her lashes.

His tongue trailed across her cheek, then traced small circles of fire in her ear, her neck, her hair. "You're all I'll ever need."

"Yes, I am."

"We've wasted so much time," he said.

"What's time to us? We have forever." Her fingertip trailed down his cheek.

"Forever," he agreed.

His lips were now slightly touching hers. It sent her crazy with longing.

She flung her arms around his neck, and claimed him with an intensity that startled them both.

His hands moved with new urgency down the curves of her body, and she arched sensually following the movement of his hands. "I can never love you enough," he whispered. "Never."

And as he kissed her so tenderly, Glory knew she had, even though his princely crown was slightly crooked, found her Prince Charming.

About the Author

Iris Leach lives with her husband Michael in Wandin in the Yarra Valley, a small community around 50 kilometeres from Melbourne, where they grow grapes and make delicious wines. She likes talking with her friends, movies, knitting, and reading romance.